Ice Cold Alice

by

C. P. Wilson

First published in 2017 by Bloodhound Books

www.bloodhoundbooks.com

ISBN: 978-1-912175-13-0

Dedication

For Alice

"The history of men's opposition to women's emancipation is more interesting perhaps than the story of that emancipation itself."

– Virginia Woolf.

Now...

1

"It's about time you got your arse in gear," he growls from his chair. Remaining silent I bow my head, chin to my chest. Chopping carrots, I have my back to him. The chair screeches across the tiles and he rises to his feet. Fists thumping the table top, he demands, "How long is that gonnae be? Fuckin' starving here."

"Not long now, Mike," I tell him quietly.

I can feel his eyes regard me for a few moments. Lighting a cigarette, he blows the smoke out forcefully.

"You sound strange; you'd better not have a cold coming on."

"Just allergies," I reply.

"Good," he barks, "Can't be doing with you being off your game just now." He returns to his chair. "Your hair looks different," he accuses. "Who you trying to impress?"

I force cheer into my voice, "No-one, Mike." The air becomes stagnant with threatened retribution as he mulls over my reply. I decide to break the silence.

"Would you like a beer?"

He snorts his derision at me. "Took you long enough to ask."

Placing the chopping knife onto the counter-top, I keep my back to him as I reach into the freezer.

"Beer's in the fridge," he cuts in. "Idiot."

"Oh, I put one in here a little while before you came home, love. Got it nice and cold for you."

"Good."

Keeping my chin tucked in low to my chest, my face obscured by my red hair, I'm the image of contrition. I hand him the beer without opening it.

Mike stares at the can in my hand, incredulous. "What am I supposed to do with that?" he asks.

I let the can slip from my fingers. His eyes follow it to the tiles, widening as the can splits upon impact, sending a spray of beer scooshing around the kitchen.

When he looks back up at me, I watch his face through strands of my hair. Morphing from surprise to a grotesque anger tinged with joy, he stands, pulling his belt from his waist.

"Dearie me. That was unfortunate." He sing-songs the words. The bastard is delighted to be given an excuse to punish me. Before he strikes, I lift my chin, showing him my face for the first time since he arrived home. My right hand is already in motion. Our eyes meet and the shock breaks his glazed predatory leer. "Who the fu-"

Sliding six inches of cold blade into his neck, I shove him roughly back into his seat, turning the blade in his neck to widen the gash in his carotid artery as he flumps onto his rump, a marionette with his strings cut.

Mike's eyes are wide and fixed on mine as I clamber to sit astride him, on his lap, a leg at each side, pinning his jerking legs. His belt has fallen to the tiles; his hands claw at his own slick neck.

"You're not. . ." He coughs blood tinged mucus.

Withdrawing my weapon from his neck, I give him *that smile*. The one that makes them tip over into unbridled fear, or rage, depending on the man. The arterial spray redecorates the walls. My eyes flick to the blade for a second. Noting that the edge is still intact, I plunge the tip into his right eye.

He screams. The sclera of his eye slides down a few millimetres on my knife tip.

"No, I'm not Sonia," I say quietly.

Sonia is gone. Despite the mortal wound in his neck, the mad woman on his lap and the blade in his eye, hatefulness kindles once more in Mike. He can't stand that *she's* out of his reach.

"She's not coming back, Michael," I tell him. "Don't bother with the tantrum, you don't have the strength anyway." I nod across at the blood-splattered fridge.

My words are wasted; he's already slipping deep into shock. The arterial spray from his neck has died to a throbbing squirt in time with the slowing beat of his heart.

Disappointed at the speed of his death, I pull the weapon from his eye which flops onto his upper cheek; a thick mishmash of cords and vessels snaking into the socket. Most of the ice-blade is wet now, its structure beginning to disappear. Unwrapping the leather straps from around the handle, I stand and place the now-slippery weapon onto his lap as one might a precious gift.

Mike forgotten, I make my way through his home, retrieving two mics and a little camera from their hiding places. I mentally check that all tasks have been done and all items are accounted for. *Devices, leather strap, dead guy.*

Clawing irritably at an itch under the wig, I remove Sonia's clothes and stuff them into a carrier bag, along with the leather thong from the blade's handle. Stood in only black leggings and long-sleeve T, I shiver upon opening the front door. The cool darkness rushes into the heated room as I leave, stirring the iron blood smell around the room then sucking it out into the darkening night. I watch my breath condense on the air and wish I hadn't left my jacket on the bike. *Never mind.*

"Bye, Mike." I wiggle my fingers at him mockingly in a dainty wave.

Stepping out into the Edinburgh dusk, I breathe the salty air blowing in from the Firth of Forth deeply. Invigorated, as I always am by the kill as well as the coastal air, I walk briskly, covering the five miles to where I left my black Triumph in the shadows of a sycamore on Grosvenor Crescent. A few minutes later I'm on St John's Road, headed for the M8. The night is alive around me. Despite the late hour, I feel vital and part of something important.

***

The warmth of my Hamilton apartment embraces me. Headed directly to the living room, I make a quick check that my blinds are closed and that the fire I lit earlier is of sufficient size and intensity. Absent-mindedly singing to myself, I retrieve the leather strapping from the ice-blade's handle and drop it into the fire. Undressing, I make a bundle of mine and Sonia's clothes. Hand over hand I roll the clothing into a tight cylinder and lay it onto the hungry flames. There they join the leather strap, followed by the wig, which crinkles and melts as it lands in the heat. Left wearing a simple plastic bodysuit, I watch the flames devour the last of Sonia. Only a faint sense of loss tugs at me. The flames swell and dance around as I unzip the plastic suit, leaving menaked aside from the PVA glue coating my fingertips. Kicking the plastic suit into the fire along with the rest, I peel the glue from my fingers one a time, tossing each tip into the fireplace.

Retrieving my devices from my pack, I spend a few moments rubbing their surfaces with ethanol before sealing them inside little Ziploc bags ready for another job. Finally, I head gratefully to the bathroom.

Almost a full half hour later, skin reddened from the long immersion in the heat and smelling strongly of carbolic soap, I step carefully from the cubicle. Catching myself in the mirror, I toss a wink then pad wet-footed into the bedroom. The white tiles underfoot throughout my little apartment feel cool and clean against my skin. The clinical detachment of the day, washed from my body as surely as any traces of Mike and Sonia's home, is replaced by the glow of expectation.

Once dried, perfumed and dressed, I grab my white iPhone from its charger and compose a Tweet. After reading it three times, I send it out via the dark web.

@Tequila Mockingbird: *Kill 17. Bully, masochist, oppressor. #Press In*

I'll update my blog later. I have around three hundred twitter followers. . . less than half that number follow my blog. Due to the ambiguity of my Tweets, I rarely get a retweet. Each of my kills is there in the public domain for any police force or government agency to stumble across. So far none has. Seventeen kills, each documented and displayed for anyone who wishes to see. Most likely anyone who bothers to read my accounts will assume that they are fiction. The work of yet another indie author desperate for discovery. A waste, really, that no-one seems to care, but that'll change.

I leave my little apartment at the Racecourse. I want to ride the Triumph again, but that's against the rules I've set for myself. The rules keep me safe.

Good thing I have other options.

My burnt-orange Ducati seems to grin at me from the garage as I step inside. *Come on, let's fly.*

Like I need any more encouragement tonight.

***

The lock slips open. Silently I slide into the hallway, closing the door of my Glasgow West End apartment gently behind me. My phone screen tells me that it's two a.m. I dim the light from the phone and point it at my feet to light my path. Choosing my stairs carefully on the ascent, I use the sides of each stair, feet in against the wall where they're less likely to creak the boards beneath. I'm good at this, the sneaky stuff. Before I reach the topmost stair, the sound of his snoring reaches my ears. Unwilled, a smile tugs at the corner of my mouth. I kill the light.

In a few paces, I'm through the bedroom door, peeling off clothes as I pad silently towards the bed. Stealth matters more than neatness, so I leave my clothes crumpled on the landing floor.

Abruptly his voice breaks my stride. "Hey, Alice. . . How did the research go?"

I enter the room. "Sorry. Was trying not to wake you."

Jimmy sits, two pillows propping him. God, he looks tired. He normally sleeps better when he stays at my place.

"S' okay. Was only dozing anyway." he smiles at me. "How'd it go? Get what you need?"

"I did, thanks, Jim," I say, truthfully.

The moonlight coming in through the window cools the room, giving it a waxy look. He never draws the damncurtains. Fussing at the tie-backs I speak over my shoulder, "Well, get back to sleep," I admonish. "You've an early shift in the morning."

Jim nods, "Aye, I will, but c'mon." He pats my side of the bed. "Spoon time."

"Just let me brush my teeth. Won't be long."

"No shower?" he asks.

"Had one at the gym," I tell him as he slips under the covers, his back to the vacant space in the bed.

"Mmhmm, good," he drowses.

A few minutes later, I curve my cool body around his, absorbing his heat.

"G'night, Alice," he mumbles.

"G'night."

2

One hand pressed flat against the frame, the other holding the latch ready, Kathy closes the front door silently. An old habit from when the kids were little, but one that she hopes will prevent her from disturbing Bobby's sleep. A creak on the stairs behind her dispels that notion.

"Hiya, love," Bobby says sleepily from the top of the staircase. "Tough night?"

Allowing her handbag to slip from her shoulder to her hand and drop to the floor, Kathy leans her back against the door. "Not too bad, love. Mostly just paperwork."

Reaching her in the hallway, Bobby takes his wife in his arms. Enjoying each other's scent and warmth, neither speak for several minutes.

"What time is it, Kathy?" Bobby asks, breaking their greeting.

"About three-thirty," she replies.

"C'mon," Bobby jerks his head towards the kitchen. "I'll make you some eggs or something."

Following her husband through to the kitchen, Kathy's creaking vertebrae remind her that she is long overdue an appointment with her chiropractor. Late nights and long hours come as part of the job, but at fifty-six years old there is a price to pay for spending hours at a desk or on foot.

Seating herself atop a leather stool at the breakfast bar, Kathy watches her husband busy himself in the fridge, fetching eggs, chorizo and some other ingredients.

"Thanks Bobby," she says.

Waving over his shoulder, Bobby replies, "No bother. Go get my phone, though, I took some pictures today you'll like."

Retrieving Bobby's phone from the counter, Kathy smiles as she begins flicking through photos of their grandson, Jack, taken at Victoria Park.

"You have the wee man over today?" she asks.

"Still do," Bobby jabs a thumb at the ceiling. "He's upstairs. I told our James to go home and get himself a rest."

Kathy nods. She and Bobby well remember the years during which their own children were babies and toddlers. A whirlwind of tasks, no space to finish a thought, and pervasive exhaustion. Despite having brought up two lovely kids in James and his older sister, Rosie, neither of them misses those taxing early days.

Whenever they look back at photos of themselves at that time, two things strike them: the kids look typically healthy and happy whilst she and Bobby looked absolutely exhausted. In their fifties now, they look fresher and healthier than they did in their thirties when the kids were demanding and life's pace was relentless.

Their James, at twenty-three, teaches primary kids locally, part-time, whilst caring for little Jack the rest of the week. His wife, Angela, is a lawyer, working similar hours to Kathy. Having grown up in a family where the main care-giver was his own father, James is a natural dad and a happy one at that.

A photo-journalist, Rosie works away nine months of the year. She checks in via Skype every other day, but months can pass without seeing her in person. Like her mother, Rosie dances to her own tune.

Kathy regards her husband as he busies around the kitchen. "That's good, love. He'll appreciate that come the morning."

"It's already the morning, Kathy," he says, gentle admonishment in his tone. The slight sting of his words reminds Kathy of old times.

Kathy steps down from the stool. Negotiating the breakfast bar, she slips her arms around Bobby's waist. Face pressed into his upper back, she squeezes him while he cooks.

"I know, love. Suppose I'm just institutionalised by now," she jokes.

Bobby doesn't laugh.

Kathy's next sentence is abruptly cut off by the voice of her grandson, calling from upstairs.

"Granda! Granda. . . I had a bad dream."

Kathy smiles. "I'll go, love."

By the time she reaches the fourth stair, Jack has spotted his gran. "Granny," he cries, setting off downstairs to meet her.

"Whoa, hold on there, Jack. You're gonna trip." Kathy quickens her pace.

Jack launches himself at her from two steps above, wrapping his little arms around her neck and his legs around her ribcage. Squeezing her tightly he giggles, "I missed you, Gran. Me an' Gramps made pancakes for supper. With syrup." Jack leans back, grinning at his grandmother. Clearly he wants her to give him a row for eating sugary treats at bedtime.

Obliging the kid, Kathy changes her expression to mock horror. "Oh! You did, did you? Just you wait until I see that Granda of yours," she says.

Jack giggles again. "It was his idea," he says.

"He is in sooo much trouble," Kathy promises, ascending the stairs, her grandson in her arms.

Jack doesn't tell her the content of the dream that had awoken him; he either doesn't want to or has forgotten, and Kathy is in no mind to stir those images. Together, they cuddle in the padded rocking chair in Jack's room, Jack with his head resting on his grandmother's breast, Kathy with her cheek resting on the crown of his head.

Kathy strokes at Jack's little calf with an index finger. Memories of time snatched with her own kids at the same age flash past her mind's-eye. Being a professional, working mother with two young children had been, for her, an exercise in impossible logistics, fatigue-management, and a tsunami of guilt. Perennially feeling as though failing at work and at home, successes felt hard to find in those days. Taking Jack regularly so that his parents might rest or actually spend time together was the least that Bobby and she could do for them.

In moments, both Jack and his Gran are asleep, arms around each other.

Bobby, mouth still chewing on Kathy's breakfast, sticks his head through the gap in the door, smiles at them huddled against each other, then returns to bed.

***

Feeling Jack's weight suddenly removed from her lap, Kathy jerks awake. Bobby is a few feet away, laying their grandson into his little toddler bed with the gentle expertise of a man who has done so hundreds of times. He lifts a finger to his mouth and nose in a *shoosh* gesture, then makes the universally recognised thumb and finger gesture for phone at his ear. Kathy sighs, prompting a knowing smile from her husband. Nodding at the door, he whispers, "C'mon."

Once in the kitchen, Kathy finds her phone laid atop the breakfast bar, a large coffee freshly made beside it.

"Thanks, love," she says, checking the time. "It's only six, why don't you go back to bed?"

Bobby scratches at his bed-ruffled hair. "Kay," he replies, "see you later."

Kathy watches her husband ascend the stairs before returning call she missed.

After two rings, Jackson picks up.

"Sorry to call so early, Kath," he says hurriedly.

"It's fine, Steve. What's the story?"

"Dead male in Newhaven. Stab wound in the neck and the eye," DS Jackson reports.

Kathy nods along as Jackson relays a series of pertinent details.

"Thank you, Steve." Kathy cuts him off once she has what she needs. "I'll meet you there in half an hour."

Then...

3

"Welcome aboard, Ms Kinney." The immaculately presented flight attendant smiled warmly at me, offering his assistance with an outstretched hand. "May I take your hand luggage for you?" he asked.

"Thanks, but I'll need a few things before I settle in for the flight."

With an extended arm, he indicated that I should proceed into the first-class area of the plane. "Please do let me know if you need anything, ma'am," he offered, turning to the next person boarding to repeat the process.

The first-class cabin seemed an alien environment, even after all the years I'd spent travelling in the *superior* section. Some people seemed to thrive in the first-class world of private lounges, waiters in the sky, quality food, and a bed for a chair. I'd never been good at allowing people to *serve me,* feeling that I was quite capable of tending to myself. Over time, though, I'd learned to submit to a modicum of assistance so as to not be rude to the staff by refusing their aid.

Retrieving my book and my heavy laptop, I chucked my carry-on up into the storage compartment. A man seated below, face in *The Washington Post*, grunted his annoyance at the resulting racket. I smiled at him sweetly, before moving through the cabin towards the bathrooms. Finding the first-class bathroom occupied, I continued to the economy section to find the one there mercifully free. I'd been running, quite literally, late as usual and hadn't managed to get to a toilet for hours.

Closing the door behind me, a woman called my name as I was making my way back to my seat. "Alice, how are you?"

Melody was one of the associates from my floor. I didn't know her well since she worked with a different department, but I had spoken with her several times at social functions. I liked her, she was a good colleague, the kind that would offer to cover for a workmate, or share a load of their work if her own were ahead of schedule. On that day, baby seat, with resting child in her arms, Melody looked like all mothers of young children boarding a flight do. Tired, and harassed.

"Hi, Melody. What on earth are you doing on this flight? Off to see family?" I asked, genuinely surprised to see her. So far as I was aware, she was still on maternity leave. I recalled that, like me, she had family in England and assumed she was visiting them.

She shrugged wearily. "Oh, I came back to work a few days ago, Alice."

Reaching out to stroke the sleeping baby's forehead I nodded at her words. In the States, it wasn't uncommon for new mothers to return to work after as little as four months' leave.

"She feels warm, Melody," I said, moving aside to allow another passenger past us.

"Yeah," she replied.

Melody looked like she hadn't slept in weeks and likely she hadn't.

"My husband is away on business. His mom usually helps look after Hayden, but she has the flu." Melody kissed her little daughter's forehead. "As does this one, but I've no choice but to bring her along."

"Oh, Melody, I'm sure you could've taken a day."

She shrugged in reply. "Not at the moment," she said, smiling in resignation. "My boss is of the opinion that I've had *enough vacation time* this year. I'm indispensable on this trip, apparently." Melody rolled her eyes forcing humour she clearly didn't feel.

Unable to keep the disdain from my expression, I shook my head sympathetically.

"What's your plans for the baby when we reach London?" I asked.

Resigned and wearied, Melody smiled weakly. "Mum is meeting us at the airport. She'll take Hayden for a few hours. . . hopefully it'll be a few hours," she laughed humourlessly.

"C'mon," I said. "I'll give you a hand getting settled."

Melody, expression somewhere between gratitude and relief as I lifted her carry-on bag, took the baby's seat, little Hayden napping uncaring as she was swung along the aisle towards their seats.

A middle-aged couple made a show of rolling their eyes and sighed loudly when they saw Melody and the baby headed towards the seat beside them. Melody, busy juggling bags and baby, was oblivious to their poor manners. I drilled my eyes into both of theirs, daring them to voice their annoyance at being seated near the baby.

A flight attendant handed Melody a parental seat belt extender as he passed. She rolled her eyes at me as he left.

"They expect me to wake a sleeping baby, strap her to my lap then return her to her seat after take-off. Pain in the ass."

"You can't just strap the seat onto the plane seat?"

"Apparently, she's safer on my lap." Melody shook her head, exasperated.

Melody unbuckled her daughter and winced as the baby began screaming in protest at having her sleep broken. The woman seated nearby tutted loudly. Melody's face was grey in pallor, her eyes circled in darkness earned from many hours of missed sleep. A new mother, she was simply spinning too many plates on too few reserves of energy. Her stamina depleted, she looked plain defeated. Something broke inside and the tears came.

I reached out to take Hayden from her. Gratefully, she handed her child to me. Instantly the kid stopped screaming, a shade of unreasonable betrayal passed over Melody's expression.

"Melody, go get some sleep," I told her, handing her my boarding card. "It's a twelve-hour flight. Sleep, have some food, sleep some more. Hayden will be fine here with me."

Automatically, Melody brushed my offer aside, with a weary wave. "That's really nice of you, but I couldn't put that onto you,

Alice." She wiped the tears from her face. Long streaks remained along her cheeks.

Holding a now sleeping Hayden to my breast, I asked her, "Why not? I'm better rested than you and I don't have work to go to as soon as we arrive in the UK. I'm on vacation, visiting my dopey younger sister. She's just had her twelve-week scan, so a little practice will do me good."

Melody's eyes flickered as the possibility of several hours rest slowly became a real possibility for her. She shook her head. "Thanks, Alice but she needs a feed and she'll need. . ."

"None of that's a problem, Melody," I cut her off. "You have some milk in your bag?"

Her expression softened. Fatigue was winning out over her objections. "Yeah," she said, "I expressed enough for the trip; the bottles are in a cool bag in the changing bag."

"Well, that's easy enough then." I raised my eyebrows in encouragement.

Guilt shaded her expression. I pre-empted her next objection by taking her hand in one of my own.

"Melody, really, this is no bother for me. I know you feel like you're letting her down somehow by even considering letting me help you out, but you're exhausted and you have a hard day ahead of you. Do yourself and Hayden a favour. Give her a well-rested mother."

Tears welled once again and broke loose to run along her sunken cheeks, forming new tear-tracks alongside the previous ones.

"Just go," I told her, kissing the top of Hayden's little head as she slept. "If she needs you, I'll come wake you, I promise."

With great effort, Melody kissed her child before trudging through to the first-class cabin and hopefully some uninterrupted rest.

Shifting the baby to a more comfortable cradle position in the crook of my right arm, I buckled us both into the chair, let out a long sigh and settled in to an unexpected addition to my journey.

4

"You look good, love," Bobby assured her for the third time. "Smart, but practical."

Kathy made an unsure expression. "The skirt though... Trousers might be better." Her tone made it a statement rather than a question.

Wrapping his arms around her from behind, Bobby kissed the side of her neck. "You look perfect, love." He turned her around to face him. "Go. Don't be late on your first day in CID."

Gathering her handbag from the bed, Kathy strode towards the door, recalled something and turned back to face her husband.

"Bobby... Thanks," she said. "Don't know what I'd do without you."

Kathy disappeared downstairs, the sound of the front door to their Leith flat clunking a few seconds later. Exasperated, Bobby sat on the edge of the bed.

Six years Kathy had been in the force, six years of volunteering for all the difficult shifts, duties and roles. Six years of apologies and cancelled plans. Six years of being completely undependable and wholly dedicated to earning a promotion to CID. Had an end not been in sight, Bobby wasn't sure he'd have had the resilience to continue his supportive role. But, here she was, twenty-nine-years-old and now a detective. Pride mingled with fatigued relief.

Allowing a long sigh to escape, Bobby let go of some stress and uncertainty along with the air.

Hopefully things will slow a little in her life now she's got what she's worked so hard for.

Pulling on his shoes, Bobby straightened his back, composed his *dad face* and headed down the hall to wake their two-year-old, Rosie.

***

Kathy tugged at the bottom of her skirt, straightening out the slight crease from having been in the car. A single deep breath and she entered the CID room. The large room, with wood-panelled, nicotine-stained walls and tightly packed with desks and cubicles, was busy with the constant buzz she'd come to expect after a few brief visits. Men's magazines, stained coffee mugs, manila folders and full ashtrays littered every surface she could see.

Ten detectives worked the Lothian and Borders Fettes department. Kathy surveyed her new colleagues, most of whom she hadn't met before today. At present six of the team were in the office. Each of their heads popped up, eyes fixing on her only to dart away without acknowledgement. Several of the men exchanged sardonic grins and raised eyebrows. An older detective, DC Graham, mid-fifties, a journeyman in Kathy's estimation based on the research she'd done on each of her colleagues, let out a hiss through his teeth.

"Stripper's here, lads," he chirped snidely.

Adolescent giggling rippled momentarily across the office. Kathy bit back an acid retort. Affecting an air of indifference, she jutted her chin at Graham.

"Aye, very good, Graham," she said flatly. Graham was one of those officers who thought that seniority meant something other than it did.

Approaching newly promoted DS Jackson, Kathy introduced herself.

Jackson wasn't much older than Kathy herself and had a reputation as a tough, able officer and a creative detective. He was also reputed to be aloof, but popular with the men in his charge and his superiors. Kathy could learn a lot from him and intended to, if she could get her immediate superior on-side.

"Kathy McGuire, sir," she said, offering her hand.

Jackson did not raise his eyes to look up at his new DC, choosing instead to jerk a sideways nod over at a desk to his left.

"There's your desk," he grunted. "There's a folder there that'll get you up to speed on your case load. DI McBride wants to see you in an hour, so get prepped."

Kathy followed his gesture. Old interview cassettes, a mountain of mouldered manila folders and a layer of dust and ash greeted her. A woman, Brenda from Middlesex, held her full breasts out from the pages of a deliberately placed men's magazine. Her new workstation desk had clearly been unused, aside from as a dumping ground, for a long time. Removing her jacket, Kathy rolled her sleeves up and set about tidying the pile of unused folders and dirt.

"When you're done there, McGuire, cup ay tea, hen," Graham shouted across the office.

Kathy raised the middle finger of her right hand in reply.

"Fucking frosty bitch," Graham mock-whispered to the detective on his right, loudly enough for Kathy to hear. "Probably a dyke."

Refusing to give him the attention or the overreaction he was seeking, Kathy returned to clearing the desk. Without looking at Graham she spoke sweetly.

"I'd imagine most women tell you that they're gay, Graham."

The office fell silent and stayed that way, aside from Kathy's cheerful whistling as she tidied her new work area.

When a space had been cleared and a clean part of the desk exposed, she sat to begin her preparation for her briefing with the DI. Aware that she had eyes on her, she glanced up to find the DS assessing her.

Unsure if the grin Jackson wore was supportive or condescending, Kathy chose to flick her eyes back to her work.

Now...

5

Tequila Mockingbird

Blog

Kill 17

Michael McKenna died tonight in his home in Edinburgh. His life was brought to a relatively peaceful end. A more serene exit than he deserved and certainly more humane than the manner in which he had treat his family for fifteen years.

A habitual abuser of his wife, Mike employed few and uncreative but expertly effective, methods of torturing his children and spouse. Mike enjoyed his family's fear. He thrived on their dread, gleefully and ruthlessly taking every minute scrap of independence or self-esteem from them. A long term gambler and adulterer, Mike McKenna created a domain in which he ruled supremely over his dependents. A man-child, Mike demanded and expected his every need and whim to be not only catered for but anticipated. Mental and physical abuse his preferred tools; vindictive domineering and manipulation his most cherished entertainment.

Across fifteen years, Mike beat his wife on thirty-seven occasions that I am aware of. During his tenure, Sonia McKenna suffered six broken ribs and numerous arm breaks as a result of displeasing her husband, or failing to foresee one of his many and unpredictable needs. Most recently, Sonia was hospitalised due to a ruptured kidney. A vicious blow delivered with gusto by a coward relieved her of an organ. *Good thing you have two ay thum,* Mike had sing-songed to her upon her return home. The damage to her internal organ was convincingly blamed on a fictional mugging in the park.

Sonia endured her husband, absorbed his blows, wilted under his deeply personal criticism of her body, her mind, her spirit.

She forced herself to survive, to remain in the family home, in order to shield her children. Her eldest, also Michael, intervened more than once. A fractured cheek bone and a broken finger did not ultimately prevent the lad die from placing himself in front of his mother time and again. Mike's control of the twins didn't always manifest in physical means. More often, emotional blackmail and fear served him fine.

I know these things about Michael McKenna because I watched him for a long time. I saw how he controlled and victimised those he should have loved and cherished.

Sonia and her children played no role in his death. I acted alone.

Mike will never harm Sonia, or anyone else, again. I opened his carotid artery and removed his eye. I looked into the remaining window to his rotten soul and watched the vindictiveness, his rage that Sonia had escaped his world, colour his last moments.

Sonia and her children are safe. Never again will they flinch from a step on the floorboards or the voice of their jailer.

Press In,

Tequila

Sitting back into my ergonomic chair, I force the padded lumbar into my spine to ease the stiffness. Gritty eyes narrowed, I scan over the blog entry, re-word a few phrases, then hit publish; my newest journal entry zips off into the ether. Chewing on my lip, I wonder idly if the blog is really just a journal anymore or if it has become something else. A statement of intent? A warning?

A sardonic grin lifts the corners of my mouth. *Not that I have enough followers for it to matter what this is.*

Regret surges in my chest. Not for Mike, certainly, but for the passing of another hunt. It isn't unlike a wedding day, the kill. Find the right man, arrange everything just so, have the time of your life and then. . . deflation. Back to the drudge of daily reality.

With exaggerated control, I gently release a long sigh. Relaxing my muscles, the exhalation takes away the disappointment along with the knotted tension. My eyes move, as though of their own volition, to the MacBook screen once again, drawn to the encrypted folder on its desktop. It's been a long time since I made two kills in such quick succession. My custom, designed initially in caution and maintained through habit, is to leave at least three months between kills. There is never a shortage of abusive spouses, and my research and preparation is meticulous, but a measure of pace and control has served well so far.

Right index finger stroking the mouse pad, I watch the little mouse cursor hover back and forth as I consider. *Move up the next kill? I have several weeks largely free of commitments. That doesn't happen often.*

I take a few seconds to complete the short series of mental exercises I use to maintain my neutrality. Killing is addictive; I will not be one of those killers who allows their base needs to compel them to foolish acts and amateurish decisions.

Mentally confirming that the notion to step up my schedule isn't being driven by emotion but by logic, the decision is made.

Conjuring the upcoming target in front of my mind's eye, I mentally skim through the abuser's details, schedule, habitual movements and routines. This one is very physical, one of the most casually-brutal I've encountered for a while. A bit of a monster really. No kids, just a perpetually cowed spouse who has had to develop a talent for makeup artistry, such is the frequency of the beatings and bruises.

Hovering the arrow over the file, I make my decision and click on the fiend's name, sending a series of programs into action that open a dozen windows and files pertaining to the abuser and the spouse. Audio and video files from inside the target's house, as well as medical records and police incident reports pile themselves across the screen.

Stevenson.

Just his name makes my hackles rise. Recalling the abuser's MO quite vividly, I ignore most of the open windows, focusing instead on the spouse. I tell myself that I'm merely boning up on pertinent details. I am, in fact, on some level, stoking my anger; granting myself permission to move up my schedule.

Recognising instantly that I've let the Stevenson kill become an emotional issue, I transfer the pertinent details of his spouse to a sub-folder, ready for sending to Seb and turn my attention to a different target. One that I'm less emotionally sensitive to.

Gary McCabe. Thirty-eight years old. His wife's medical records tell a tale of defensive bone breaks and lacerations. One hundred and seventy-five stitches have pulled and held her skin together over the years. Summoning all the required details for Mrs McCabe–personal data, physical dimensions, preferred attire, education and work history–I flick the required particulars to a waiting email draft. Attaching sixteen usable photographs for my agent to work with, I request the full package and a twenty-four-hour turnaround then send the order with a single click. Five seconds after the email swishes away a reply from Seb pings through.

Order received.

A man of few words and sometimes none at all, Seb is utterly reliable and infinitely discreet. We have a long and stable working relationship in which trust was established long ago. Quite literally I would not be the person I am today without Seb's input. Seb may be the only person in the world I trust.

Clearing the clutter of open documents and windows from my desktop, I leave two single images open. Taking only partial notice of the photos of the abuser and his dependents, I let my eyes drift out of focus and my thoughts cool. Impartially and without emotion, I analyse, select and discard the myriad of methods, timings and strategies available to me in the coming few days. Almost two hours pass, during which time I must appear a still, silent presence, staring deep into the clean painted walls of my Hamilton apartment. Abruptly my body loses the rigidity it has held whilst I consider my next hunt. Relaxing once more into the chair, my smile returns.

Searching my recent memory, my fingers move across the keyboard. The plans I've made in my head alone somehow become more real, more imminent as I transfer the dates, methods, locations etcetera into data.

6
Newhaven, Edinburgh

Squinting against the low Edinburgh sun, Kathy pushes away the useless regret nagging her over missing breakfast once again with her grandson. Focusing instead on her good fortune at the lack of traffic, she guns the engine in her Cooper S. The early hour means uncharacteristically quiet streets, allowing her to reach the cobbled hill leading to Newhaven Main Street within two minutes of leaving her family home. Scanning along the row of little white houses, Kathy pulls to the kerb inches from Steve's feet. Stepping from her car, she ignores his lop-sided grin.

"Nice parking, Kathy. Still have all my toes and everything."

"Stand somewhere less stupid then," she replies, hiding a smile of her own.

Conceding, Stevie nods towards the staircase of number six. "Interesting one for us this morning, Kathy. Male, forty-two years old, stab wound to the throat, eye removed."

Glancing to the top of the staircase, Kathy nods along, observing the bustle of crime scene officers and forensics techs through the living room window. Kathy turns her attention back to her long-term partner. "Removed post-mortem?"

Stevie's eyebrows arch. "During, looks like," he shrugged.

Kathy intimates her surprise. "Someone didn't like him very much."

"Seems that way," Stevie agrees as they reach the front door.

Nodding greetings at colleagues, Kathy picks a careful path across the living room floor, avoiding the markers and bags left behind by the forensics techs. A few paces behind, Steve traces her footsteps but manages to knock over one of the numbered markers, eliciting a scowl from the forensic pathologist, Dr Ferguson. Steve offers the doctor an apologetic shrug. Fixing his eyes on Kathy, Ferguson pointedly ignores him.

"Detective Inspector McGuire." Ferguson peers accusingly over his half-frame glasses. "Shall we begin?" His eyes dart to Steve momentarily. "Before my crime scene is contaminated any further?"

Kathy nods once. "Go ahead, Doctor Ferguson."

Ferguson does not consult his notes as he talks them through the details. A monumental pain in the rear he may be, but the man is a consummate professional.

"Victim is Michael McKenna. Forty-two years old, good health prior to his death, no records of any significant medical concerns."

"No previous criminal record, either, Kath," Steve interjects. "Guy works at the flour mill just across the road."

"Quite, Sergeant," Ferguson scowls. "If I might continue."

It's another accusation rather than a question. Stevie shrugs his permission.

"The victim was stabbed in the throat, here," Ferguson gestures at the open hole in McKenna's neck. Kathy can feel the air prickle as Stevie bites back an acidic comment.

"Tearing the carotid artery," Ferguson continues.

"Tearing? Not slicing?" Kathy asks.

Ferguson raises his eyebrows. "Exactly so," he says, placing a thumb and forefinger at the wound. Opening the ragged breach in McKenna's skin, Ferguson leans to the side, allowing the detectives an unhindered view into McKenna's neck. "Look at the vessel. Not pierced, not sliced by a sharp edge, more like it has been torn. Something rough shoved and ripped the fibres apart instead of cleanly penetrating."

Examining the wound and the exposed blood vessel, Kathy's brow creases into a frown. "It looks similar around the skin wound also," she mutters, moving closer still.

Clearly approving and enjoying his moment, Ferguson leans in to point at the wound with his free hand, shouldering Steve to the side casually.

"You're quite correct, DI McGuire. You see this tearing here and here?" Ferguson indicates the edges of the wound, the section that most likely had been the first point of contact with the murder weapon. "The same ragged tearing here as on the blood vessel where we should see a clean slice."

Kathy fishes her reading glasses from her pocket, then draws Ferguson's attention to the blood vessel once again. "Is it my eyesight, Doctor, or is the tearing different, perhaps slightly more ragged, at the vessel than the skin?"

Ferguson's lips move to arrange into his version of a grin. As close to smiling as the man gets, he radiates surprise at Kathy's observation.

"Quite so," he says jovially. "The damage has increased between the skin cut and the artery cut, almost as though the weapon had degraded somehow, or been damaged as it made the cut."

Ferguson releases his hold on the wound, allowing the skin to close partially around the gaping hole in McKenna's neck.

"Same thing here," he says, indicating the eye wound with his pinkie.

"No murder weapon then?" Kathy asks over her shoulder.

"Na," Steve replies. "No sign of anything that may have been used for this."

Ignoring the exchange, Dr Ferguson continues. "I suspect that, despite the unusual cuts, we will not find metal or wood fragments in the wound."

Removing her readers, Kathy catches his eyes. "You have a theory?" she asks.

With a shrug, Ferguson replies, "Of course. Look here, Detective." With a circular motion, Ferguson indicates along and under the lower eyelid of McKenna's damaged eye. "Note the similar ragged damage to the eyelid?"

Kathy nods once.

"As with the previous two wounds, but as is consistent with the blood vessel, the tearing to the tissue here has changed once again, seemingly confirming that the weapon was itself being damaged by its use."

Kathy chews at her lower lip as she processes the implication of Ferguson's words. For once, the doctor is content to let her reach her own conclusion.

Pointing at the neck, Kathy talks herself through the events. "So, our killer stabs McKenna in the neck here, the weapon tearing as much as stabbing." Kathy's hand, holding an imaginary blade, moves to the eye socket. "The killer withdraws the weapon, sending that arterial gush spraying," she juts her chin towards the fridge, "and then pushes the same weapon into the eye socket, causing an even more ragged injury and the victim's eye to vacate the socket." Kathy's eyes move involuntarily for a moment to the eye resting stickily on McKenna's cheek.

Ferguson nods along as she re-enacts the murder. When it's clear that she's paused in her monologue, he interjects, "Good analysis, Detective," he offers with genuine admiration.

Lost in visualising the moments of McKenna's death, Kathy only faintly hears him speak.

"There's very little damage to the room or anywhere else on the victim's body," Kathy says, her eyes moving across the seated body of McKenna and his surroundings. "The killer was calm, unhurried," she adds, absent-mindedly. "The victim didn't put up much of a fight. Perhaps he didn't have the opportunity to."

Ferguson folds his arms across his chest, before adding to her thoughts, "Two precise stabs: one to kill, the other to torment. No signs of a struggle or any defensive marks on the victim."

"No forced entry either," Steve interjects, eliciting a grimace from Ferguson.

Mind busy processing the scene, eyes scanning the kitchen, Kathy acknowledges them with a silent nod. Following a few moments' silence, she speaks softly.

"He didn't even stand up."

"Aye. Seems he knew the killer," Steve observes.

Turning to face Ferguson, Kathy asks, "Has the preliminary forensics turned anything up?"

Ferguson's eyes sparkle. "Absolutely nothing, Detective. No blood other than the victim's, no footprints that don't belong to shoes owned by someone who lives at this address, no weapon. Just a few red hairs that most probably belong to the wife."

Catching a subtle nod towards a nearby shelf, Kathy follows Ferguson's gesture, her eyes meeting a photo frame. A couple smile from the picture. McKenna and his wife, arms around each other. It looks recent. McKenna appears a larger man in the shot than he does slumped in his kitchen. His wife holds him and herself in a manner that Kathy finds unsettling. Two kids, late teens, fill the picture alongside them. Standing apart from their parents they look uncomfortable in a way only teenagers can. Something itches at her mind then leaves without recognition.

"Where is she? Where are the kids?" Kathy asks over her shoulder.

"We don't have a clue," Steve replies. "Nobody has seen her since she left work the night before McKenna died. The kids are both at university, one in Strathclyde, the other in Glasgow. Initial enquiries haven't been able to contact either."

Kathy nods.

"Always the spouse, Kathy, in nit?" Steve says.

Ferguson snorts his derision. "Only if the wife is a professional killer with a unique weapon that we can't identify." Shaking his head, Ferguson moves away from them, turning his attention to the living room.

"Dick," Steve spits after him half-heartedly.

"He is a dick," Kathy agrees, "but that doesn't make him wrong."

Then...

7

Having earlier said reluctant goodbyes to Melody and Hayden at Heathrow and promising to meet up with them in London during my vacation, I stepped out of the doors of Edinburgh Airport to find an unseasonably warm September day welcoming me. With it having been over six months since my last visit home, I'd expected a repeat of the late winter/early spring weather I'd left behind. Turning my face to the sun, I mentally soaked up a little of its energy, fortifying myself for the day to come.

Casting a glance around the pickup area, I searched the faces present, as well as in the windows of unfamiliar cars, for my sister. An hour passed, during which I'd patiently smiled to myself at how characteristic it was of my younger sister to run late. By the ninety-minute mark, my smile had vanished. In a mild strop, I hailed a taxi and spent the journey to Nicole's house sour-faced, the sun's glare through the window now merely an annoyance.

***

Rapping the front door hard with my knuckles, I forced my irritation aside and composed my expression into one of passive concern. During the short taxi ride, I'd got over the surge of anger at having been left standing in the terminal and almost convinced myself that Nicole and I had miscommunicated the pickup time, or that my sister had simply been having a bad day.

The door swung inward on my second knock. Nicole stood, eyes wide, concern evident.

"Alice, I'm so sorry," she blurted immediately, stepping forward to take me in a tight hug. Her little baby bump pressed against my abdomen as she held onto me. Any lingering annoyance I'd harboured evaporated. We were together, my little sister and I, after far too long a spell apart. Nothing else mattered.

Reluctantly, we broke apart. Placing a hand on her bump, I asked, "How's my wee niece or nephew baking in there?"

She smiled awkwardly, throwing me again with the oddness of her expression.

"The baby is fine. Come in, Alice," she smiled at me, taking my hand to lead me into the hall. In contrast to the appearance of her home on my last visit, the hallway was startling in its cleanliness, as was the living room. The rooms were minimally furnished with little or no ornaments or photos adorning walls or shelves. The place looked like a show home. The smell of bleach permeated the house.

"You're turning into Mum," I said indicating the pristine look of the room.

An unfamiliar expression passed over her face so quickly I almost didn't notice it. *Guilt? Fear?* Whichever, it was something I'd never seen her express in such a way before, but brought a pang of old memories all the same. The realisation made me regard her a little more closely as she moved around the room, shifting my bag and adjusting a few magazines on the coffee table. Something, perhaps lots of somethings, had changed in her demeanour.

"Yeah," she joked half-heartedly. "Bottle of bleach a day, so I suppose I have turned into our mother. I'm putting it down to pregnancy hormones. Tea?" she asked.

"Coffee," I replied with an eager nod.

"Long flight?"

"Lovely flight, actually," I informed her without elaborating.

Nicole led me through to the kitchen. Whilst she prepared our drinks, I watched her, becoming more uneasy with each entirely new and subconscious little mannerism or habit she displayed. Her appearance, whilst not greatly changed, was just. . . off somehow. Her hair, much more neatly cut, sharper than usual. Where once her fingernails would have been shaped and painted to perfection, they were now clipped and bare of adornment.

Practical. Observing her clothes, minimal makeup and the hair, I realised that she was as obsessively clean as the house itself.

Her eyes darted about the room as she spoke or went about her task, drawn by little *flaws* she absently fixed in passing. Everything she used – mugs, tea and sugar jars, even the milk in the fridge –were all returned precisely to where they came from after use, labels lined up.

Watching her, my formerly-nonchalant little sister, the kid I'd screamed at to clean our room, the young woman who had delighted in tearing carefree through life, I felt my chest tighten.

"So, what happened to you this morning?" I asked pleasantly.

Nicole's face darkened. Her eyes narrowed and cast downwards and then she recovered her composure.

Forcing a lightness into her voice, Nicole wiped at the worktops as she spoke, her back to me. "Oh, Darren and I had a bit of an argument this morning. I just lost track of time, that's all."

"Mmhmm," I replied, sipping at my coffee.

"All sorted out now," she added.

Nicole had been with Darren for a couple of years now. Finding him disengaged and a little aloof, I didn't particularly like the kid, but I didn't have any real reason to dislike him either. At twenty-three-years old they were a little too young to have moved in together, but with a childhood like the one Nicole and I experienced, her rush to set up a home of her own was understandable.

"Is it a problem, my being here this week?" I asked her bluntly.

"No," she blurted. "It's just that, well, I told Darren I'd have something done and I hadn't, so he was. . . a little disappointed, that's all." Noting the confusion on my face, Nicole added, "I just had to fix it, that's why I couldn't make it to the airport on time, okay?"

Nicole was becoming distressed. Placing an arm around her, I pulled her close, observing that her eyes had reddened.

"I'm sorry for prying, sis. It isn't like you to react like this."

"Och, I'll be fine in a minute." She broke off, returning to her endless wiping of surfaces.

Not feeling like letting it go, I pressed her.

"What's going on here, Nic?"

Nicole's forced neutral expression broke. Tears snaked at pace down her cheeks. All veneer of normalcy disappeared.

"I keep on screwing up, Alice," she spluttered through the tears. "At work, at home; I can't do anything right."

Stood in the centre of the kitchen, one arm hugged around her body, the other laid over her small baby bump, Nicole was forlorn, isolated and desperate, a slender shade of her usual self.

Where was my breezy, perennially excited sister? I'd gleaned nothing of her current mind-set during our daily telephone calls. What had I come home to?

Following a moment of silence broken only by her sobbing, she looked up at me through a curtain of her dishevelled hair and tears.

"I can't do anything right anymore, Alice." She was shaking.

Taking her in my arms once again, I realised for the first time how small she seemed. The change I observed was not physical; she'd lost a little weight despite the pregnancy, but not a worrying amount. Physically she seemed almost normal, but something had diminished, lessened her. Something, or someone.

"What the hell's going on here, Nicole?" I demanded.

Feeling her back straighten I loosened my embrace. She wiped at her mascara-streaked tears. Her eyes struggled to meet my own.

"Darren," she said. Her glance darted fearfully down. "He's been under a lot of pressure at work and the pregnancy has been hard for him. . ."

Dread and sickness in my gut, I cut her off.

"What's he done," I demanded coldly.

Nicole's entire body stiffened. Watching my little sister process relief at having told me, then instantly shift to fear that she'd done it broke my heart.

Caught in between the need to ask for help and her desire to cope alone, Nicole stood quiet for a spell, struggling to decide what to say. A practiced flatness entered her expression. The lightness of her tone, the easy dismissal of her words, stunned me.

"It was only one time and it was mostly accidental."

8

Responding to Kathy, DI McBride pursed his lips. A high-pitched squeaking noise from his teeth made Kathy wince. He at least appeared to be considering her placement request. With a final squeak, McBride unclenched his lips, forming a flat line.

"Why Jackson?" he asked. "There are several good DCs you could work alongside. Graham has mentored our last three junior detectives and made a fine job of it."

McBride raised his eyebrows. His expression gave Kathy the impression that he was challenging or testing her.

"I'd be perfectly happy to work under whomever you choose, sir, but I figured that my skill set and DS Jackson's would make for a good match."

Kathy stifled a relieved sigh as McBride gestured for her to continue.

"DS Jackson is one of the few officers in the Lothians who has had experience in tracking a serial, sir."

McBride nodded his assent. "That he is and. . .?" he prompted.

"My degree was in criminal psychology and criminology, sir. I've attended numerous courses and night classes during my time in the force to enhance my knowledge and skills in this area. Quite frankly, I feel that working with Jackson would be best for my development."

Leaning back into his chair, he observed her for a moment without speaking.

"After Jackson's job, are we?" he asked, his tone challenging.

"No, sir," Kathy replied instantly. "I'm after yours." She attempted a respectful grin. "After you move on to your next role, of course, sir."

McBride grinned slightly at her forthright manner. He'd clearly expected a long list of half-truths and politically correct justifications for her request.

Then the smile vanished abruptly. "And what does DS Jackson get out of it?" he asked plainly.

Kathy decided to take a gamble. "He gets to work with me," she said wryly.

McBride laughed loudly, starting Kathy slightly.

"Why the hell not?" he asked no one. "Alright, DC McGuire. Consider yourself assigned to Jackson. He'll mentor you for the next six months, we'll reassess then."

McBride nodded at the door. Kathy whirled around to exit.

"Send Jackson in here, please McGuire. No sense in waiting to give him the good news."

"Will do, sir."

***

Clearing the last of the clutter from her desk, Kathy reached into her bag. She placed a framed photo of herself with Bobby and Rosie onto her desk.

A derisive snort came from one of her colleagues. Kathy chose to ignore it, focusing instead on one of the files DS Jackson had labelled '*active cases*'.

A cursory scan through the files made it clear that Jackson had offloaded all the cases no one else wanted onto the new DC. Kathy smiled inwardly. She'd expected to have to work all the crap duties: collating reports, cross-checking cases and basic filing. It came with being the new person on the team and had nothing to do with her gender. Having moved on quickly from each of her previous teams and shifts, she'd become accustomed to beginning at the bottom again.

A few months of grunt work and hopefully she'd get handed something a little more challenging.

Abruptly, Jackson crashed into the office, his face three shades of purple. Kicking at a chair in passing, he strode directly over to

DC Graham. "Gimme the mentoring guidelines, Graham," he barked down at the seated detective.

Responding to Jackson's aggressive tone, Graham's brow furrowed. He looked like he may rise to his feet and get into it with his superior when his eyes suddenly widened.

"You've been assigned McGuire," he blurted. His braying laughter followed.

Jackson held his hand out. "Just give me the guidelines, Craig," he growled.

DC Graham's smile flattened but did not vanish altogether.

Handing the document to the DS, he looked around to bask in his colleagues' shared reaction. Each of them, fearful of the boss's rancour, kept their eyes fixed to their work.

Jackson slapped the document onto his desk, before rounding on Kathy.

"McGuire. We're working on the Leith Links murder. Move your arse."

Jackson slung his coat over his arm and barrelled through the double doors without waiting for her. Kathy concealed a smile. Carefully closing the file she'd been working on, she refrained from making a snide remark to Graham as she left the office. The slight spring in her step was plain to see.

Jackson was waiting in the corridor outside and Kathy almost clattered directly into the skulking DS. He placed a hand rigidly in front of himself. Connecting with her shoulder, he halted her momentum solidly. Jackson's face hadn't got any less purple in the fresh air of the hallway. Three large veins throbbed in his temples and forehead.

Kathy composed a neutral expression.

"Flutter our lashes at the DI, did we?" he accused, leaning in to press himself into her personal space.

Face passive, Kathy ignored his intrusion. "Not at all, sir. The DI simply agreed that our skills would be a good match."

Kathy moved to sidestep around the DS and found him back in her path. His face contorted into a sneer. He spat the words at her. "Fucking hell. Two minutes in the door and McBride is dancing tae your tune."

Kathy took a step back. Folding her arms across her chest, she nodded at him insolently to continue. Anxious to vent, Jackson obliged.

"So, instead of doing the grunt work you should be doing, you're now partnered up with me on all of my cases. What fucking use are you? You're expected to earn this, McGuire, not get a free pass 'cause you've got tits."

Despite her easy ability to brush off these types of remarks and encounters, even turn them to her advantage, something in his tone destroyed Kathy's cool exterior. Pressing her face closer to Jackson's she got into *his* space. He immediately backed away, just a fraction, but it was a concession.

"I'll do both, DS Jackson." Kathy forced calm coldness into her tone. "Anything you put on my desk will get completed on time, or ahead of, to the best of my ability. I don't expect or want any special treatment."

Jackson's left eyebrow raised. His thoughts were inscrutable.

Relaxing his rigid posture, he reduced the intensity of his glare.

"Right then." Jackson spun around to exit the building. "Hurry up McGuire," he called over his shoulder.

Letting her taut frame relax, Kathy let out a long breath before following her new mentor on their first case.

Now...

9

"I'd just rather you stayed at your own place for a few days, Jim. I'm sorry if that's a problem." I sip my coffee in the gap he leaves silent. The faintest sound of an exasperated sigh transmits over the connection.

"It's not a problem, Alice. I just hoped that we could maybe spend a little time together now that your research phase is over." The line returns to silence for a few seconds. "We don't see that much of each other at the moment, and that's fine, but normally we have a few days when you're off the back of a project before you start writing."

On another day, I'd placate Jimmy, go for dinner, or visit the cinema, but today his whining is starting to grate. "Yeah, I just don't have the time right now. Stay at your own place and I'll call you when I have more time on my hands, Jim."

His annoyance is palpable over the line. In a strained voice, he signs off. "Have it your own way, Alice. You always do."

Rolling my eyes, I check off a mental box placing Jimmy in the 'past the easy-going phase' section of my life.

A long sigh escapes me and I set my coffee onto the little wall I'm sat on. To anyone bothering to notice me, I'm a blonde, dressed in a business suit, just another worker-bee, people-watching during a break. From under my large-framed sunglasses, I watch the specified left-luggage locker in Buchanan Bus Station, awaiting confirmation or a refusal of my offer to Mrs McCabe.

Nearby a man, I guess mid-thirties, strolls along, a pushchair with a content and chatty toddler grinning lopsidedly and rubbernecking at the people walking by. The man's stride, his gait and the manner in which he chats idly back and forth with his child tells me everything I need to know about him. This is the beauty of people-watching. These moments, shared publicly between strangers, on display for any who might care to witness.

I grin over at the child, a little boy, as he catches my eye and return his eager wave. His dad's eyes catch the exchange and his lips form a similarly lopsided grin to his son's. So few people engage with children they don't know these days. It's a shame. I smile at the boy's dad, mouthing *he's great* at him. He looks tired, as one would expect of a father with a child his son's age, but his face radiates contentment and pride that someone else sees his son for the indomitable force of eager life he is.

The quick exchange triggers a surge of contentment in me, dispelling any lingering annoyance from my conversation with Jim. Such is the power of a moment with a stranger, especially a child.

A glimpse of a blue coat in my peripheral vision pulls my eyes back to the left-luggage locker in time to find Irene McCabe standing a few feet away from the designated locker. That she is here bodes well for a positive choice. Of the thirty-six abused spouses I've contacted to date, twenty-five have accepted and followed through on my invitation to come to a locker or other such drop-off. A simple text from my white phone.

A new life awaits you if you have the courage to take it. I'll make sure that he never finds you. Locker such and such, at this or that location. Combination: 234997

Of those twenty-five, eighteen have gone on to accept my offer; most recently, Sonia McKenna who almost collapsed when she examined the contents of her locker. The remainder walked away. Out of respect for their choice and regardless of how disappointing it was, I did not reattempt contact with any of them. None of the spouses who declined my offer have spoken to anyone of it, most likely from fear of their abuser discovering their momentary foray into free-thinking. In my lighter moments, I attribute their silence to some sort of sisterhood. This is a fantasy, though. They are merely scared.

In her locker, Irene McCabe is discovering a rucksack containing an Irish passport bearing her image and a new name. A wallet containing an open-ended first class ticket to Amsterdam and five-hundred euros. A driving licence, social security number, credit cards and details of where, in a locker in Schiphol Airport, she will find other documents she may need to enable her new life. The Schiphol locker also contains details needed to access a bank account in Luxembourg holding two-million euros and accessible only to a person bearing the new ID. The money will leave the account if not claimed within thirty-six hours.

Finally, the same letter I always send, personalised for her alone:

Dearest Irene,
I've watched you struggle, fight and suffer at the hands of your husband. Your dignity and will to survive is immense. Your capacity to endure, staggering. However, the depths of the strength you've accessed to make it this far are not infinite. You will crumble under his abuse eventually.

Life was not meant to be this way for you, Irene. Remember the girl you were, the dreams you had. Try to recall a trace of the desire and ambition you once held before he convinced you that you didn't deserve those things, that you were incapable, that you are less than what you really are.

The will and heart and your capacity for living the life you once envisaged are still there. Snatch onto the threadbare tendrils of who you were and pull them close. You don't have to believe that you can be that person you meant to be, you just have to believe that you are not what he has made you. You can take this new life I've left in this locker for you and make it what you wish it to be. You can live it, one day at a time, as you see fit.

You do not require anyone's permission to do so. You don't even have to think ahead to what or who or how. You merely have to decide you want to, then take the contents of the locker and start over. Right now, this very minute.

You can never return. Your husband will never find you, I will make sure of that for you, and I will punish that man for how he's brought you to his heel; for how he has stripped away at your self-esteem and confidence to a sliver of what you once possessed.

Believe this: you have the strength. You can be who you were, or you can be anyone else you wish to be free of your abuser. You merely have to choose. Whatever choice you make, I shall of course respect your wishes.

All my hopes and dreams for you in your new life.
Press In,
Tequila.

One hand to her mouth, the other hugged around her battered torso – an almost universal habit of abused spouses – Irene slams the locker closed. Taking a few paces backwards she props her rear on a bus shelter seat. Her legs look unsteady. My eyes narrow as I assess her reaction. I'm too far away to hear her sobs or see the tears, but the little suppressed movements of her shoulders convey her shock to me. For several minutes I watch Irene McCabe go through the same thought processes and resulting gestures as so many other women I've invited to a new life. A little elderly woman passes by, stops to offer a word of support then continues on her way, a backwards glance for a final check of Irene before she rounds the corner out of the station. This is common. When someone is crying, more often than not a passer-by reaches out to comfort them. Generally, it is a woman doing so, occasionally a child. Rarely do men stop to comfort a crying woman.

Irene's breathing looks to be slowing. Her back straightens. This is a good sign.

The briefest of nods to herself tells me her decision is made. She has searched herself and found what remains to her of her old self. Her true self. Is there enough there to give her the belief she needs to move forward?

Three minutes later, I drain my coffee and watch Irene remove her new life from a battered and dirty locker. Irene looks around her nervously before shouldering the backpack full of opportunity and dropping her old handbag into a nearby bin. This single act visibly empowers her, almost as though she is discarding the pain of a decade. Her back straightens and her face forms an expression it hasn't worn in years. Determination.

The smallest of pauses and she steps lightly onto the airport bus, leaving her handbag, her coat and her old life behind. I retrieve my Triumph and head west on the M8, wishing Irene the best with all of my heart.

Ninety minutes later, I watch Irene step from a French Connection store in Glasgow Airport dressed in a tastefully smart business-like skirt and blouse. She has already purchased a new phone using her brand-new identity, as well as makeup and a novel to read. Standing at the side of the main thoroughfare through the terminal, surveying the crowd of people around her, I can see her confidence is already beginning to re-emerge. New clothes, a modest amount of makeup but still more than she's worn in years and the smell of a new start on the breeze and this flower is eager to blossom once again.

A hint of a smile playing at the corners of her mouth, the woman who had been Irene McCabe merges with the throng of commuters, headed for her flight to a new world. I watch with satisfaction and genuine pride as she disappears into the crowd. The instant she leaves my line of sight, my thoughts ice over.

Okay, Mr McCabe. Time to pay.

As I leave the terminal, a call on my black iPhone scratches at the coolness of my thoughts. A quick glance at the screen tells me that it's my editor, Sam. Unwilling to allow whatever she's enquiring after to break my focus, I send the call to answer phone and switch off the phone. Whatever Sam wants isn't urgent, she's in the final days of editing my latest novel and unlikely to need any vital input. Besides, we've worked on so many projects together by now, Sam already knows what I'm likely to recommend and is merely enquiring out of courtesy.

I remove all thoughts of books and editors from my mind and slip back into the cool certainty of preparing for the hunt. Clean purpose replaces everything else. Atop my bike, I slice through the night air, a lioness, fixed on my prey.

10

Rising from her chair, Kathy stretches the kinks from her back and neck whilst sighing loudly. Steve juts his chin in a *what's up* gesture.

"Just getting tired of going around in circles." she smiles at her colleague.

Stevie nods his agreement. "Witness statements aren't really getting us anywhere, are they?"

Kathy shakes her head. "Too many contradictions to be useful in giving us a revealing narrative. No one who knows Sonia all that well has seen her since before the murder, but. . ." Kathy bobs a nod at her screen, "the neighbour states that he saw her enter the McKenna home shortly before Mr McKenna arrived there on the evening he was killed."

"So?" Steve shrugs.

"So, the neighbour didn't get a clear look at *Sonia*. He only saw her from behind as she entered the house. Good description of her clothes and hair. She looked the correct height, even said she moved like Sonia, but he was twenty feet away looking at her back."

Puffing his cheeks out in a show of exasperation, Stevie nods his agreement that the witness was useless.

"So, we're left with a body, a whole lot of blood, a very clean crime scene, no reliable eye-witnesses, a missing wife and kids and a mystery weapon."

Steve raises his eyebrows, a mocking smile on his lips. "At least this isn't a dull case," he offers.

Kathy's reply is interrupted by her phone. She makes do with raising a mid-digit at her old friend.

Steve makes a drinking gesture with his hand, offering her a coffee. Kathy nods her thanks, before turning away to speak into the phone as Steve heads to the kitchen. By the time Steve returns, Kathy has finished her call and is pulling on her jacket.

"I'll take that to go," she says, taking the mug.

"Something come up?" he asks.

"Ferguson has something 'interesting', or so he said."

"Forensics?"

"Aye," Kathy confirms. "And something on the body apparently."

"Want me to come along?"

"No thanks, but would you chase up young Gilmour, see if he's got anywhere on the comparison search?"

Steve nods his agreement.

"Maybe our luck is changing, Kathy."

Kathy shrugs. "Got to sometime. This bloody case, something just. . ." Her voice trails off. Steve gives her a moment, but she wafts at the air dismissing the thought.

"Right, I'll see you later," she says over her shoulder as she goes.

***

Ferguson is sat at his desk finishing off his lunch as Kathy enters his office. A glass pod, part of the lab, it's impeccably appointed and as one might expect, forensically clean. Fetching a little desk vacuum from an out-of-sight drawer, Ferguson, mouth full, nods a greeting towards her as he cleans the crumbs from his workstation. Swallowing his food, he attempts a smile, exposing spinach on his teeth.

"Thank you for coming, DI McGuire. I have several things I'd like to bring to your attention."

Gesturing towards the lab, Kathy says, "Anything you can give us would be a huge help at this point, Doctor."

Ego flattered to his satisfaction, Ferguson wipes the corners of his mouth with a paper napkin, before leading Kathy through the main working section of the lab.

Seating himself at his PC, Ferguson beckons Kathy to lean in to view his screen. A high resolution set of images from the McKenna home begin to appear, which Ferguson scrolls though, presumably searching for particular shots he's bookmarked for her. Selecting an image of McKenna's neck wound, Ferguson swoops a finger around the edges of the wound.

"Around here, Detective." He leans aside to allow Kathy a closer look.

"The tear cuts we noted at the scene?" Kathy leans in closer.

"Yes," Ferguson replies before spinning the wheel of his mouse to zoom in on the wound. "Note the discolouration of the flesh where it's puckered at the seams."

Kathy's eyes narrow as she scans the image. "Slightly blackened?" she offers.

Ferguson nods. "Most likely frozen," he offers, turning his chair to face her.

"Frozen?" Kathy asks puzzled. "From the morgue?"

"Absolutely not," Ferguson responds. "Having looked at a sample of the cells under the microscope, it's my opinion that something very cold was used to make the cut. It's the only explanation for why the cells look like this."

Ferguson switches to an image taken of the cells from his microscope.

"This is the sort of tissue and cell damage one generally sees with frostbite," he states. "Whatever made the cut was cold. Very cold. Cold enough to freeze and burst the cells on contact."

"That's the reason for the discolouration?" Kathy asks.

"Yes. The skin had essentially defrosted by the time we attended the scene. That's the reason for the discolouration at the edges of the wound. Ice crystals damaged the tissues and the blood vessels."

Kathy rubs the back of her neck, an old tension-relieving habit formed during many hours spent poring over evidence.

"Why would the killer use a frozen knife?"

Ferguson shrugs. "I don't think our killer used a knife at all."

Selecting three pictures on his screen, Ferguson lines them across the monitor, pointing to several sites in sequence.

"Here, on McKenna's collar."

Sitting back he waits for Kathy to finish his observation. Tiring of his constant need to have her demonstrate her deductive reasoning Kathy's reply is tart, "It's wet."

Seemingly oblivious to Kathy's tone, Ferguson swipes across the next two images. "Water was also found here and here."

Pointing out another, larger damp section on McKenna's lap and a puddle under the chair he died in, Ferguson allows her the time to take in the images before continuing.

"We tested the fluid expecting sweat, or perhaps tap water or some such. What we found was pure, distilled water that had been frozen and subsequently melted. We've found no such stores of water in the McKenna home."

Suddenly aware of an aching tiredness in her legs, Kathy leans her backside against Ferguson's desk. "Doctor. . . Why would the killer bring ice to a murder?"

"I think that the ice was the murder weapon, Detective," Ferguson states plainly.

Kathy's eyebrows arch up. "That's a new one."

"Indeed." Ferguson is looking up at her from his seat but still managing to view her over the top of his glasses.

"Is that even possible?" she asks.

With genuine and uncharacteristic consideration, Ferguson pauses for a few long seconds before replying, "Perhaps a blade could be crafted from ice, but it'd have to be done with precision and no small degree of technical skill. I'll see what I can find out about crafting ice objects and if it's possible to put the sort of edge on an ice blade that'd give us a cut like those." Ferguson nods past Kathy to his screen.

"Thanks, Doctor. I'll get our young DC Gilmour to add the new information into his search. Anything else?"

"Yes, as it happens. Follow me please."

Leading Kathy to his main work bench, Ferguson retrieves an evidence bag from a nearby drawer. Placing it into her hand, he watches her hold it up to the light and manages to not make her feel like she's being examined for once. A single very long, very red hair rests, sealed inside.

"Sonia McKenna's?" she asks.

Ferguson shakes his head. "Synthetic, but a similar colour to Mrs McKenna's hair. Almost a perfect match."

"So my witness *did* see a woman fitting Sonia's description enter the house."

Ferguson shrugs. "Not for me to say, but *someone* was in the McKenna home wearing a very good quality hairpiece."

Kathy grins. "You've made my day, Doctor."

The flat grin returns to his lips for a split second.

"Oh, I'm not finished yet, Detective."

Pulling an A4 envelope from the same drawer, Ferguson hands it to her. Kathy pulls a handful of photographs from inside, holding each of them up in turn to examine them. Each of the photos shows a section of wall from inside the McKenna home. A few dirty marks, some that look like rings, have been lit and photographed by Ferguson's technicians.

"I'm not seeing what's relevant here, Doctor," Kathy admits eventually.

"My tech believes that those are suction marks. She checked the diameter and is analysing traces of material left behind. No saliva unfortunately, just a little of the rubber and plastic from whatever was attached."

Taking the photos from her hands, Ferguson flips past several, stopping at a shot of the front window, which shows a clear circular mark in the upper left corner of the pane. Smaller than the ones on the walls, it is nonetheless more clearly visible.

"My tech's best guess at present is that these were surveillance devices. Most likely they'd been in place for several months and were removed on the night of the murder."

Humour dances in Kathy's eyes. "Doctor, you are my favourite person today and by a long, long way."

Ferguson manages to look both affronted and pleased by her remark.

"Incidentally, Doctor. You may want to check your teeth."

Then...

11

"It was only one time and it was mostly accidental."

Judging by the change in Nicole's expression, which morphed from forced-dismissal to wide-eyed fear, my own reaction must've conveyed all the horror, shock and cold anger I was feeling inside. Not all of that anger was for Darren.

"Tell me everything, Nicole. Right now." My voice, every inch her older sister speaking, left her in no doubt that she'd best do as I say.

Sitting with her face in her hands, she eventually looked up at me, tears once again streaking her face.

Disclosing the recent events of her life to me was clearly the very last conversation she'd planned to have with me this week. Despite her obvious fear and reticence, a needy and grateful remnant of my little sister looked out from this broken woman's eyes. Conflicted, Nicole looked utterly dejected at that moment.

"We've found it difficult adjusting to being a couple who live together Alice," she said.

Nicole scanned my face for a moment, gauging my frame of mind. I bit back a vapid comment and gestured for her to continue.

"The first few months were fine, no, better than that. They were good. We did the same things we always had: movies, pub, walks in the park on lazy Sundays and we got to come home to each other. It was great."

The way she spoke, it seemed like she was recounting events that had taken place years before, instead of merely a few months.

"After a few weeks, little things began to make us bicker." She wafted a hand dismissively. "You know, all the crap that comes with running a home. Washing, dishes, cleaning. Darren's never had to do that sort of thing before; his mum did everything for him and his younger brother."

"So he expected you to do the same," I interjected.

She confirmed this with a tight nod. A little of her old spirit shone in her eyes for a moment.

"Initially I told him it'd have to be different in his own house. We'd divide the tasks and I'd do the ones he found most difficult, at least at first."

A resigned expression passed over her face.

"How long did that last?" I asked bitterly.

"Less than a week," she admitted.

"Over the last few months he's gone from being completely unaware of what's required in a house, to demanding utter perfection in every room."

I shook my head as though to dispel my confusion.

"Why?" I asked, genuinely puzzled.

"When he began to ignore the housework, I turned into the classic nag. I needed him to do his share, I wanted him to care. He grew more resentful of me, as I did of him. He lost his temper during an argument."

"He hit you," I finished for her stonily.

Nicole shook her head. Her eyes darted away, unwilling to meet mine.

"No. Not that time. He was furious, though. He ranted about how if I loved him, I'd look after him properly. He called me a lazy bitch, told me I'd be a useless mother to our child as I couldn't even look after him to a decent standard."

My fists clenched tightly enough to turn the skin white as I listened to my sister.

"What did you do? How did you respond?"

A flicker of her old self showed once again in a lopsided smile.

"I waited a few days. . . and then I wrecked the place," she said, forcing the smile to linger. "Emptied the hoover all over the sofa and carpets, sprinkled it like fairy dust throughout the house. Pulled out all the food from the cupboards and left it lying around the kitchen. Creased up all the clothes I'd ironed earlier in the week. Took a dump in the toilet and didn't flush."

My chest swelled: this was more like my feisty, strong sister. Abruptly her forced smile vanished.

"When I came home, he was sitting on the edge of the couch. He wasn't angry. In fact, he didn't look emotional at all, Alice. He was just. . . vacant, shut down."

I nodded along, encouraging her to continue.

"Without a word he punched me in the face, then held me down on the carpet. He choked me, Alice, until I passed out. When I came to, he was standing over me. He only said one thing to me. 'Do that again and next time I hurt the baby'."

Overcome, Nicole placed her face in her hands. I was fighting deep rage. At him, for the mental torture he'd had my sister living under, for daring to touch her. Anger at her that she could let this happen; that she would endure living like this and say nothing to me, after everything we had survived as children.

With great effort, I made the anger a small thing inside me, allowing my reason to return. As though she'd felt the shift in my mood, Nicole looked up at me.

"I feel so small, useless. I feel like a coward, Alice," she pleaded.

"That's exactly how he wants you to feel. Trapped, alone, insignificant," I told her. I cupped Nicole's cheek in one hand. "Well, you're none of those things and we're not going to allow this cowardly little prick to turn you into any of them."

I lifted her chin up, forcing her to look at me.

"You hear me, Nicole? We didn't come this far to allow this to happen."

A lowering of her eyes betrayed her thoughts.

"I can't leave him, Alice."

My anger cresting once again, I strode away from her only to whirl around, hands offered pleadingly.

"How can you not?" I accused. "No, there's no way you're staying in this house," I railed. "Not one more day."

"I'm not having my child grow up without a father!" she blurted suddenly.

"No father is better than one like him," I said. "You know that better than most, Nicole."

I watched her straighten her back and lift her head. She was making her mind up, solidifying a course of action. I knew my sister, if I allowed her to reach this conclusion, accept this life, she'd bloody-mindedly and doggedly continue on that path until it destroyed her. Compelling myself to composure, I changed strategy.

"Nicole, you know that I've been doing really well since I moved to San Francisco," I began.

Wondering where I was going, her eyes narrowed.

"Well, let's just say that money is no issue. I can move you out there with me. We can set you up in an apartment nearby, or you can even live with me. We can hire help so you can get back to work if you want, or just be a full-time mum to the kid."

She shook her head. I cut her off before she could object in words.

"I know this guy," I said. My hand strayed absently to my diary inside my bag. "He's an investigator, of sorts. . . It's kind of difficult to explain, but he does a lot of different tasks for my company and he's become a friend these last few years. He manages everything for me, my money, legal issues, he's what we call a *fixer*. This guy can literally give you a whole new life, Nicole."

Shaking her head, Nicole stood, taking me in a hug. Her weak voice was growing in strength as she committed herself to staying put.

"I appreciate that, Alice, but I'm not running away again."

"It's not running away," I blurted angrily. "It's taking control of your life, refusing to be a victim." I patted my handbag. "I've Seb's details in my diary. We can call him now if you want to."

Her eyes hardened. "I'll decide for myself," she said plainly.

"Next you'll be telling me that he'll change, that it'll never happen again, that it was your fault for provoking him," I accused her. "That's what women in this situation always do."

"You don't know him, Alice," she said flatly.

We stood looking at each other in silence for several long moments, Nicole's face set in grim determination, my own a mask of steely will. Our glaring was broken by the sound of keys in the lock of the front door.

All stoicism gone from her face, the cowed wife appeared again, pleading with me.

"Please Alice, just let this go. Don't get into it with him."

The living room door opened outwards as he stepped into the room. I drilled my eyes into my sister's.

"Fuck that," I spat the words.

12

"Bobby, I can't do this again. Not today."

Bobby crossed his arms, closing himself off from her. "And I can't keep holding this family together alone, Kathy. I'm desperate here."

Watching her strong husband practically beg her for help, Kathy felt her determination waver. *Perhaps I could just cancel this* . . . Bobby saw it in her yes, his own widened in gratitude. *No!* she decided. He saw in her eyes too and reacted badly.

Storming out of their bedroom, Bobby stomped downstairs with heavy feet. Kathy heard him reach the bottom and pause for a few seconds, most likely composing himself before he entered the kitchen where the children were eating supper.

Guilt was her entire world at times like these. Another trip away, another series of meetings. More time alone for Bobby and the kids. Rosie was missing her mother badly, the kid had become so used to saying goodbye to Kathy that she'd become hardened to the routine. Little James was barely over a bout of the sickness virus. Bobby, of course, had been the one to nurse him through those last few vomit and fever-filled days. Both of them were utterly drained and needed her.

You said things would change when you joined CID. It's been three years now and you're worse than ever. Operation McGuire comes before everything.

Words spoken in anger echoed in Kathy's ears.

Padding out into the hallway, Kathy listened with keen ears as Bobby made his way around the kitchen below, placating the kids.

His voice light, his tone flippant, he used his *dad voice* to hurry the kids along, encourage them to eat.

"Where's Mum?" Rosie asked her dad.

Kathy winced. Nothing got past hat kid. She must've heard them arguing.

Bobby's voice strained with forced levity.

"Oh, Mummy's going away tonight, she'll be back in a few days."

Rosie fell silent. Kathy could picture the stoic expression on her five-year-old daughter's face as she buried her disappointment at her mum leaving once again for work.

"Mama!" James shouted cheerily from his high chair.

"Well, it's the weekend," Bobby said hopefully. "We can visit Gran and Gramps, maybe go to see the winter wonderland down in Princes Street gardens?"

"Don't wanna," Rosie grumped. "Mum said she'd take us," she added.

From above, Kathy could imagine her husband steel himself, perhaps swallow a fruited, bitter remark. He never spoke badly of her in front of their kids, regardless of how frustrated or annoyed he'd become with her frequent absences.

"Mummy would love to come, darling. We'll go again, just the four of us, next time she has a day off."

Rosie snorted. "That'll happen," she mocked.

A loud sob broke from Kathy. Covering the noise quickly with one hand, she ran to her bedroom, tears staining her vison.

For several very long minutes, Kathy cried and punched into her pillow silently.

Failing at home, never feeling that she was able to give enough at work, Kathy was falling to despair and resigning herself to always being a let-down in both of her lives. She had spread herself too thinly, it was simply too easy to fail at everything. Her husband and children resented her more everyday. Her colleagues continued to make her work life unpleasant. She departed her home, having rebuilt her self-esteem and shored her determination each and every day. Guilt, frustration, failure and endless exhaustion were consuming her. Something had to give. Kathy had stopped caring where success came from, home or work. Either would do, but she needed to feel it somewhere.

Kathy washed her face twice, adjusted her clothes and her hair, threw herself a sardonic, humourless smile in the mirror and built a wall around her heart that'd allow her to leave her family yet again, right when they needed her most.

***

Half listening to DC Graham talk incessantly at him from the passenger seat and doing a passable job of appearing to listen to his Old Firm diatribe, Jackson took the junction for Cathedral Street. Descending the off-ramp into Glasgow, their car raced past the Royal Infirmary and the Strathclyde University buildings.

From the rear seat, Kathy scanned the exteriors as they whipped past, trying to bring to mind a vague notion of who she'd been or how she'd felt when she'd been a student there.

Life had changed so very much. With innate confidence, Kathy had known exactly who she was in those days. She'd also known exactly what she wanted from her life and a firm plan on how she might attain that life. Bobby had been the very image of self-possessed assurance. A journalism graduate, he had the kind of easy-going nature that Kathy needed to balance her occasionally consuming drive to succeed. Nothing flustered Bobby McGuire. He was the type of man who had looked at each new day as an adventure. Bobby saw opportunity everywhere. His career had taken him into writing articles for a sports magazine, allowing him the opportunity to work from practically anywhere. He'd travelled much in their early days together, whilst she ground out shifts as a junior uniformed officer. Until Rosie had come along and he'd chosen to limit his time away to be home for her and support Kathy.

The bitter exchange of that morning with Bobby had weighed heavily on her all day.

Seeing the still-lit buildings, students inside studying hard, late on a Friday, she considered how so very different from those younger versions of themselves she and Bobby had become.

"If you keep sighing like that, I'm gonna put you out at the next red light, McGuire," Jackson spoke over his shoulder.

"Sorry, Sarge," Kathy said half-heartedly.

"Time ay the month," Graham said to no one.

Jackson and Kathy both ignored his remark.

"When we get there, McGuire, I want you to take lead in the presentation."

This was news to Kathy.

"You're sure, sir?"

As he pulled the car to a stop at a red light, Jackson's eyes moved up to survey her from the rear-view mirror. "Unless you don't feel ready."

They'd been prepping for the presentation to the CID officers at the Pitt Street HQ for two weeks. Jackson was to have been lead, with Kathy merely providing a supportive, research role. That Jackson had chosen this moment – a half hour before they were due to present – to switch roles, smacked of throwing her under the bus.

Kathy's eyes narrowed as she took a moment to consider. Jackson was not an easy commanding officer to work under and whilst he hadn't been particularly supportive in the years she'd worked with him, he hadn't actively attempted to sabotage her work either.

Choosing to view the late shift in roles as a positive development, Kathy smiled warmly to Jackson via the mirror.

"I'd be delighted to, Sergeant. Thank you for the opportunity."

Jackson offered her a single curt nod before the lights changed and he resumed driving.

Graham remained uncharacteristically silent, but his furtive shifting in his seat conveyed his amusement.

Kathy took her mind back over the last few weeks of prep she'd been involved in. Jackson had insisted throughout the process that Kathy should involve herself and absorb all aspects of the presentation they would give on serial killers and their methods. Having assumed that Jackson was simply being his overly-demanding self, she had of course researched and revised diligently.

It seemed that the sergeant had intended to hand the presentation to her from the very beginning. So intent had she been on driving through the work with her usual forceful gusto and her now customary chip on her shoulder, Kathy had been blind to the obvious development opportunity Jackson had handed her.

The simple opportunity she'd been given to show her skills and knowledge alleviated a portion of the stress she'd laboured under. As the car pulled to a stop in Pitt Street, Kathy stepped from the rear seat, smoothed down her skirt and resolved to regain her lost positivity.

Now...

13

As always, my Hamilton apartment helps keep me in that predator's zone required before a kill. The clean white walls and wooden floors, as much part of the preparation ritual as any of the tasks I meticulously perform, bathe me in a clean sense of purpose.

My next target, McCabe, lives in an apartment complex in Ruther glen, just outside of Glasgow. With a Tesco supermarket nearby, a car dealership and mostly open ground and car parks, there aren't many homes to overlook the building. The Tesco supermarket is open twenty-four hours but rarely sees a customer between two and four a.m. As I'm unlikely to be seen, I don't plan on any elaborate disguise on this kill. A brunette wig with an unremarkable cut, minimal makeup with a memorable feature, a prominent nose in this case, courtesy of a prosthetic. Simple black leggings and long-sleeve T cover my customary under-attire of a plastic zip-up suit to prevent trace DNA as much as possible. I won't require to dress as the spouse on entering the home on this kill. If I'm seen, I'm just another anonymous building tenant.

In my underwear, seated at my breakfast bar and freshly scrubbed with carbolic soap and rough hand pads to remove most of the dead skin on my body, I listen to the Suicide Squad soundtrack as I paint the uPVC glue onto the fingertips of my right hand. I find rap motivating but not overly stimulating. A good punch line seems to agree with my mental state during a kill prep.

Whilst the glue dries, I check the freezer for the third time. Finding a neat row of my custom blades lined in their moulds along the freezer shelf, I run a fingertip along the edges determining the keenness of each one. It isn't easy to get exactly the right edge honed on a weapon made of ice. Finding the exact mould and temperature has required hundreds of hours of trial and error and many hundreds of discarded efforts. A surge of pride threatens as I smile at the perfect ice blades laid out in my freezer. Each one is precisely moulded and made from the purest distilled water as to leave none of the characteristic chemical profile one might expect from untreated tap or bottle water. Perfectly balanced and with a leather thong serving as graspable material, they feel like a part of my hand now, despite their coldness to hold, or perhaps because of it.

Closing the freezer, I check the fridge for the third time too. My cool bag and ice packs, for the transport of whichever blades I select, are at the perfect temperature to ensure minimal damage to the weapons. There's no risk of melting within the window I've allotted myself, my weapons are too solidly composed and frozen at minus thirty to ensure this. However, the edge can form a slight sheen of moisture if not attended to in transport, making the rough edge I spent so many hours perfecting less able to penetrate flesh. Recognising a further surge of pride in my craft and preparation, I shove away at it. Pride is a distraction on kill days and one likely to lead to mistakes.

Closing the fridge door, I pad barefoot over to my work satchel. The size of a mini-iPad and made of tough acrylic weave, my pack contains only those items I'll need for the kill. Lock picks, my white phone -turned off - and a backup metal-bladed knife that is to be used only as a last resort. The small cool bag holding my ice blades will complete my pack.

Feeling that the glue is dry I return to the breakfast bar to paint the fingertips of my other hand. Absent-mindedly and for no reason I'm aware of, I reach out to my laptop, the clean one and bring up my blog.

The little notification icon with its red alert causes me to do a double-take. On a normal day, I may have two or three notifications. Today more than seventy-five thousand await my attention. This is not a distraction I can allow, not today. With no small amount of will, I close the lid of my laptop, dial the volume on my music to maximum and expel from my mind all questions as to why my blog has suddenly sprung a new life. Tomorrow. . . or perhaps later tonight, I'll deal with it then. No time for distractions.

Once the glue tips are dry, I zip myself into the plastic underclothes and complete my makeup, before pulling my over clothes on. Blades packed, I head for the garage and my Triumph, allowing a faint trickle of excitement at riding the bike to surface for the journey to Glasgow Green.

***

With the Triumph hidden in a cluster of large shrubs I take off across the park, following the pathways, at an easy pace, somewhere between a brisk walk and a lazy run. In a short time, I crest the little hill leading down Dalmarnock Road and the large Tesco store slips over the horizon. I've encountered no pedestrians at all on my journey; even Glasgow is dead in the early hours of a Tuesday. Of the three cars that pass me en-route, only one driver took note of the late-night jogger. Clearly amused by the crazy lady running in the middle of the night, she'd blown a large vape cloud out the window as she passed, paying me little mind. The smell of sweet cherry floated into my lungs from her window.

Stood in the parking lot to the rear of the apartment building, I scan along the facing windows from the shadows of a young oak tree, just tall enough to lend me cover. Of the several hundred windows, only a handful glow with soft light to indicate the presence of a night owl, gamer or insomniac. Mercifully, McCabe's third-floor apartment's windows are in darkness. The car park itself is deserted, aside from my own presence.

With no sign of movement at any of the lit windows, I palm my lock picks and steal my way quickly to the security door. A thought tickles me and I check the time. Just gone four a.m. Grinning, I press the service button. The door pops open instantly. Slipping in I close the door gently behind me and light-foot it up the staircase towards McCabe's apartment. Excitement crests in my chest. I squash it instantly.

The staircase lights are set to low for the night time. Thank God for eco-savers. Any shadows I make as I pass nearby windows should go unnoticed. A few feet from McCabe's door, I notice a faint glow at the bottom of the doorway. His hallway light is on.

Is he awake? Waiting up for Irene? Pacing angrily at her absence?

There's no way for me to know. As I saw no light from the living room window, no flicker of the TV or lamp shining from the bedroom window, I take a chance that he has merely gone to bed and left the hall light on.

Sliding my tools into the door's lock, I work the mechanism, slowly but confidently, bringing its disparate parts into alignment. A soft clunk informs me that I've succeeded.

Returning the picks to my pocket, I crouch at the doorway, partly listening for tell-tale creaks on floorboards from within, but mostly so that I can retrieve one of my ice blades from its cool bag. As my hand closes around the leather-wrapped handle, the frosty sensation seems to spread up from my hand permeating my entire body and soul. If I were a shark, my eyes would be dilated and glazed with the smell of the blood to come. As it is, I merely wear the predator's grin.

A gentle, exploratory push opens the door a crack. An invitation to anyone who may be waiting to challenge my entry. Without incident, I make a larger slice between door and frame and slip into the apartment's hallway, closing the door silently behind me with my butt.

On my haunches, blade low at my side in a loose grip, I cock my head to the side and close my eyes, trying to get a sense of where in the apartment McCabe may be. The doorway to the bedroom on my right lies open, door swung into the darkness of the room. No sounds of sleep come from within. As I'm considering whether to enter the room or slip towards the living room, the toilet flushes in the bathroom, making my decision simple. Spidering my way silently into the bedroom, I take position behind the door, awaiting McCabe.

The hall light clicks into darkness a moment before he enters his bedroom. McCabe doesn't bother to close the door behind him before he flops face-first onto his bed.

A dozen strategies and options flicker through my mind for a fraction of a second before I settle on one. In two paces, I reach the bed, place a knee roughly onto his upper back, the other across the back of his right shoulder. As he shakes the fug from his drowsing mind and the adrenaline races through both of us, he manages to twist his head around to look up at me. The bastard actually smiles, like it's some kind of midnight fantasy he's woken up to. I take that notion from him and the smile from his face by sliding three inches of ice into his right kidney. McCabe discovers that the kidney is one of the most exquisitely painful places in the human body and lets loose a satisfying scream which I stifle, by shoving him down into the bedding with my knee. In an attempt to raise himself from the bed he jerks wildly, mostly with his neck. He's a big guy and given another few moments will manage to throw me off, despite the pinning hold I have on him. If he gets the chance.

Withdrawing my ice blade, I move up to his neck, just above where my knee is now struggling to hold him down. A quick flick of my eyes to the tip confirms that the blade is functionally intact. Sliding it into the skin at the back of his neck I focus on the blade's path, pushing it down with both hands on the hilt. Ignoring his rising torso, I concentrate on slicing through the muscle layer and avoiding the thyroid artery. Ultimately, his struggle to rise aids the knife's progress. A little skip of the weapon as it scrapes over the thyroid cartilage into the soft tissue beyond tells me I'm on target. Abruptly, he stops pushing back against me and ragdolls down onto the bed. His face has dropped, the cheeks look melted. I've severed the nerve that controls. . . controlled the muscles there. The abrupt end to his struggle tells me his spinal cord is damaged enough to prevent communication with the muscles below my cut.

Gently, like a lover withdrawing, I slide what's left of my blade from his neck. I take a moment to place the abuser into the recovery position, lest he choke on any fluids gathering in his throat.

Leaving McCabe on the bed, I enter the en-suite, unwrapping the leather thong from the weapon's hilt a turn with each stride, before tossing my melting blade into the sink. Briefly I reflect idly on how hot human blood actually is when released. The surrounding tissues my ice blade severed and parted held enough heat to melt most of the upper edges of the blade, leaving a blunt instrument where a surgically sharp tool had been.

Stowing the sodden leather in my satchel, I retrieve another ice blade from the cool bag. Regarding myself for a moment, I note the joy present in my eyes. On another night, I may chide myself on the lapse in my detachment. Tonight, I go with it.

"Be with you in a moment, Gary," I sing-song through the open door.

McCabe groans something unintelligible in reply. It's going to be a long night for him. For me, it'll be over all too quickly.

14

Kathy shifts in her chair as DC Gilmour arranges his notes and boots up his computer, prepping for his report. Eyes circled beneath in darkness, rimmed in red, the kid looks tired. He works hard, but it isn't work that has him looking like he's been dragged through hell week with the Royal Marines. Kathy checks her watch: eleven a.m. Most likely he's been in the station all night.

"Fuck," he exclaims, throwing a hand out in a failed attempt to catch the coffee mug he's just knocked from the desk. Immediately his eyes move up to meet Kathy's. "Sorry, ma'am," he stutters.

Kathy rises from her chair. Negotiating her way around the desk, she lays a hand on each of her junior officer's shoulders.

"Lewis, it's fine and I've told you before, call me Kathy. Jesus, even DI McGuire would be an improvement."

Gilmour attempts a smile that doesn't reach his tired eyes. He bobs a nod and turns back to prepping.

Resuming her seat, Kathy asks, "How is the wee man?"

A genuine smile lights his face this time.

"He's good," Gilmour beams. "Keeping us busy."

"What is he, four months now?" Kathy asks. "Tough time for a first-time parent, Lewis."

Gilmour's face creases. He looks like he wants to say *you're telling me?* Instead he simply nods. "Had croup the other night, gave us a bit of a fright."

"That is a scary one the first time you see it," Kathy agrees. "He doing alright now?"

"Yeah," Gilmour confirms, grateful for the show of support. "Just been hard getting him back into the routine, y'know? Especially at night."

Recalling the illness in her own kids very well, and the stage of parenting he's at, Kathy nods along, allowing him to vent a little. "It'll pass, Lewis. It'll get easier."

Smiling the sad, disbelieving smile of a man trapped in the daily hell of having a new baby, Gilmour clears his throat, signalling that he's ready to report.

Recapping all they've discovered succinctly – the synthetic hair, the water, the ice weapon theory, as well as eye witness statements–Lewis does an admirable job of summing up the case to date as Kathy patiently listens. When Gilmour has completed his summation, Kathy asks, "So what has your research turned up?"

A dip of Gilmour's head to the side betrays him. He has information he's hesitant to relay.

"Lewis?" Kathy prompts.

As he moves to reply, Steve clatters through the doors into the office. Three cups of coffee balanced in his hands, he puts one down for Kathy, another for Gilmour and plonks his backside onto the edge of Kathy's desk.

"Christ sake son, you look shite," he observes without judgement.

Gilmour nods his thanks for the coffee. Ignoring his sergeant's assessment of his appearance, he recovers the thread of his conversation with Kathy.

"I've been searching the police database UK-wide for cross-references to any of the elements and evidence of our case. So far, I've had three hits on distilled water found at murder scenes and . . . fifteen men murdered alone in their homes, with their spouses having disappeared around the time of the murder."

Kathy's eyebrows rise in genuine surprise. "Fifteen?" she asks. Gilmour nods.

"Have any of the spouses turned up since?" Steve asks.

"Not a single one of them," Gilmour says.

Kathy leans forward. "Do any of the forces or detectives involved suspect the women?"

"Despite their disappearance, in each case the families have not been considered serious suspects. At least, not for very long."

"Families?" Kathy asks.

Gilmour shrugs. "Some of them," he checks his notes. "In four instances, children of varying ages have disappeared along with the spouse."

Kathy sits forward in her chair, horror etched on her face. "The families, the spouses are being killed too?"

Gilmour shakes his head. "I don't believe so." Spinning his chair around, he activates the office's smart screen. Steve and Kathy share an ominous look as they wait for the projector's bulb to heat up illuminating the screen.

A bullet-pointed list of items, which Gilmour proceeds to talk them through, comes slowly onto focus.

Selecting the first item, Gilmour brings up video footage of a woman in a hat entering a bus station, proceeding to a locker, and then disappearing from shot. "This is Stacey Hopkins, twenty-eight years old, from Birmingham. Her long-term boyfriend, one Jason Fleming, was found stabbed through the chest, a wound that severed his aorta, killing him at home. He died four hours after this footage was captured. Stacey's whereabouts at the time of his death are unknown. His body went undiscovered for two days, until their cleaner found him. This was seven years ago. No trace has been found of Stacey aside from this footage."

"She didn't board a bus?" Steve asks.

Gilmour shrugs. "The local police don't think so, but they can't know for sure. She was seen entering the station and then no other sighting of her was caught. They checked CCTV from the rail stations and airport also. Nothing. She did not buy a ticket, not on any of her cards at any rate. Stacey's credit and debit cards have not been used since she vanished."

Kathy makes a winding gesture telling Gilmour to go on.

"No distilled water at this scene; a kitchen knife belonging to the home was identified as the murder weapon. No usable prints and no DNA from anyone who couldn't subsequently be eliminated as a suspect."

Gilmour pauses for a moment, giving space for questions. As none are forthcoming, he continues, closing Stacey's file he clicks on the second item on his list. An image appears of an elderly man in the morgue, gaping neck wound filling the screen.

"This is Edward Creaney. He was killed in Manchester last year. Very similar wound to our Mr McKenna, as you can see. The Manchester Police discovered distilled water and synthetic hairs at the scene. Mrs Creaney has been definitively eliminated as a suspect, but has also vanished. Her grown-up children, one late forties, the other early fifties, have not heard from their mother since the murder. The family describe themselves as *not a close family*."

Gilmour spends the next fifteen minutes relaying details of murdered men found in Scotland, Wales and England over a period of eight years. Some show traces of distilled water at the scene, while others have a clearly identified murder weapon in evidence. Several of the cases he describes had synthetic hair fibres at the scene. All of them involve a missing spouse and sometimes children.

Kathy, nodding along as her junior officer conveys his findings, holds a hand up to stop him. "So, all fifteen you've discovered have missing family members, some have the distilled water and some not, and some have synthetic hair fibres but most don't," she summarises. "That about it?"

"Yes, ma—DI McGuire," Gilmour confirms.

"Have you a summary of the evidence in each case?"

Gilmour nods before bringing up a table showing the evidence of each case, all lined up.

Kathy's eyes narrow as she processes the data. She can feel Steve doing the same.

"This is good work, Lewis," Kathy murmurs. Abruptly her eyes fix on a section of the smart board before flicking to Lewis. "There's a lot of compelling crossover between these cases and genuinely convincing narrative for a serial." Kathy's eyes transfer to Steve, a silent exchange and not a pleasant one crackles between them. Gilmour pretends not to notice and waits for the *but*, which doesn't come. Kathy's eyes return to the screen.

"The killer, if it is the same killer, seems to have killed with whatever was close to hand during the earliest murders before changing to what Dr Ferguson thinks is an ice blade."

Ignoring a derisive snort from Steve, Kathy continues.

"However, the manner in which the men died – quickly, no defensive wounds, clean, life-ending cuts and stabs – is consistent with one person being the killer."

Gilmour lets out a breath Kathy hadn't been aware he'd been holding. Clearly he'd been hesitant to disclose his theory on a serial killer being responsible. They are so rare in Britain it's not an idea that comes easily to most cops.

Steve stands to point out a section of the board.

"The time and location of each death is fairly consistent too, Kathy. Always during the early hours, always when the victim is alone at home."

"There's something else, sir," Gilmour adds, addressing Steve.

Rolling his eyes to Kathy at the youngster's insistence on formality, he juts his chin at the constable. "Well?"

"I had a gut feeling about something, so I did a little digging."

Looking uncomfortable once again, Gilmour flips a few images across the screen, coming to rest on the photo from the McKenna home that had unsettled Kathy during her visit.

His eyes turn and his voice lowers as he speaks.

"I grew up in a house where domestic violence was a part of our lives." Gilmour's eyes drop in embarrassment. Kathy sits forward. Gilmour's face has reddened. He is aware that both she and Steve already know this about his upbringing, but long-ingrained emotional responses still rise up in response to his disclosure all the same.

"I know a battered woman when I see one," Gilmour says softly.

Her own feelings when viewing the picture of the couple reflected, Kathy urges him to continue.

"I felt the same way when I saw that photo, Lewis. Go on."

Gilmour's eyes lock on Kathy's. Gratitude emanates.

"I contacted Social Services and requested medical records for all of the women in the cases I've identified. So far, I've had returns from eight. In six of those cases, the missing spouse had visited hospital or received support as a result of domestic violence, but pressed no charges against the husband."

Steve let out a long low whistle. "That's one hell of a motive."

"For the wives?" Gilmour asks.

"No," Kathy interjects. "Someone else."

"You really think this could be a serial, ma'am?"

Reluctantly, Kathy nods. "Yes and one with a skewed sense of justice."

His report done, Gilmour sags a little, prompting a smile from Kathy.

"You've done some great work here, Lewis. Now go home."

"But ma'am. . ."

"But ma'am nothing. You're off-shift. Go home, rest, spend some time with the baby and give that wife of yours a break. I don't want to see you back in here for forty-eight hours. Clear?"

"Yes, ma'am." His reserves spent, Gilmour sags further.

Observing Gilmour leave the office, Steve leans across to appropriate Kathy's untouched coffee. "Kid's good, Kathy."

"Yes, he is," Kathy agrees. "I wish he were wrong though." Reaching across to pick up the landline, Kathy throws a humourless grin to Steve. "I'll call the DCI, you get the Chief Super."

Steve fetches his own phone from his pocket one-handed whilst raising the middle finger of his other hand in thanks for Kathy's generosity.

As the phone rings, she offers, "I'll take the press conference if it makes you feel better, Steve."

Then...

15

"Fuck that!"

The words barely past my lips, I whirled around to face Darren as he entered the room. Never particularly bright or inventive, he was possessed of a confidence that his intelligence or deeds did not justify. At well over six feet tall, he'd filled out substantially since I'd last spent any time in his company. His face and eyes, often disengaged from activity or discussion around him, now blazed with purpose. His once unobtrusive manner had morphed into a stormy presence that filled the room with blackness.

What had happened to him? Was this always who he'd been?

His quick eyes assessed the mood instantly. Turning them to me, he managed to inject spite and boredom into his expression.

"What have you done to upset my girlfriend?" he accused.

Nicole took a light grip on my upper arm.

"Please, Alice," she said quietly.

Darren's eyes darted to her for a moment. A warning of punishment to come? Indecision froze me for several long seconds. Darren mistook my hesitation for weakness. Stepping around me he placed his arm around Nicole, in a gesture that was more about ownership than protection.

"I think you should leave," he said, his mouth a flat line.

Observing my sister, so small, so vulnerable, completely within his mental and physical grasp, my resolve returned.

"I'm not going anywhere without my sister," I asserted.

Intending to take her hand, I moved towards Nicole. Darren shifted his feet a few centimetres to his right, enough that his large frame blocked my way.

"Get out the way, Darren," I warned him.

His breath warm, he laughed in my face, a humourless laugh filled with disdain. Ignoring him, I reached around to snatch at Nicole's hand.

Darren moved quickly. Grasping my wrist, he snarled at me, "Get the fuck out of my house."

Any fear I could've felt for a man like Darren had left me many years ago. Still in his grip, I pushed my arm, continuing to reach for Nicole.

Stubbornness rather than reason guided me. Darren tightened his grip substantially. Twisting my wrist, he threw me to the floor effortlessly, my arm wrenched painfully by the act. Continuing his movement, Darren spun around to face Nicole. With a solid shove to her chest, he sent her sprawling back into an armchair.

"Sit there and shut up," he warned her.

Returning his attention to me, he chose to goad rather than attack.

"Your family always go on about how alike you two look. *Like twins, rather than ten years between them,*" he mocked in a voice resembling our mother's. "Well, you ain't like twins. You're a miserable, hatchet-faced old cow." He jabbed his finger into the air between us to punctuate. "You're such a stuck-up little cunt, Alice," he spat at me venomously.

Rising to my feet, I resisted the urge to cradle the arm he'd wrenched. I brought myself directly into his personal space, shoving the hand of my unhurt arm against his chest, which didn't budge him a millimetre.

"And you're a pathetic little coward," I accused.

Aside from the slight flicker of a bitter smile, his face kept the same disinterested, superior expression. "Now, get out of my way, I'm taking my sister somewhere else."

His voice lowered. "You're not taking *her* anywhere," he hissed.

Nicole, eyes widened in stark horror, sat behind him. She mouthed desperately at me to leave.

Long hours spent absorbing blows and insults from our father's hands and mouth, years protecting my little sister, a lifetime of saying *no* to a man who wanted to control me surged to the fore, causing bilious acid to rise in my throat and adrenaline to course through my frame.

Before I knew I'd decided to do so, my right foot thumped into his groin. He fell and fell hard, crumpled into a foetal position. I stepped over him, spitting onto his contorted face as I did so.

In my resolve to remove Nicole from *his* home, I said only one word to her as I reached for her hand. "Move."

Her hand absently protecting her abdomen, her eyes moving between Darren and my face, Nicole's expression undertook a subtle shift. My sister decided in that moment to come with me. Relief rushed through me, doubling my resolve to remove her from this man's house.

I took her hand and hauled her up roughly with my uninjured one. She screamed her warning a half second too late.

Darren looped a large arm around my neck from behind. With the power of one who has been wronged, in his own mind at least, he twist-threw me across the room where I crashed through a little coffee table. Despite rolling onto all fours almost instantly, I did not see his follow-up blow coming. A vicious stomp to my head sent me crashing onto my back. Part-way between consciousness and oblivion, I fought the closing darkness, wishing I could just let go. I watched him stalk towards my sister.

"You fuckin' bitch," he roared at her, betrayal was acid in his words.

A heavy fist striking Nicole in the abdomen was my last half-conscious image of them before I passed out.

16

Invigorated, Kathy stepped out into the chill evening air and onto the sloping pavement. A satisfied smile settled and she mentally flipped through the key moments of her presentation. Throughout the session, with four Chief Supers, two Sergeants and a DCI from Inverness present, she'd conveyed the necessary details and insights and responded to their probing questioning with a cool and informed demeanour. She'd felt in charge, certain. She'd been the focus of the room, the person each of those in attendance turned to for clarification or to verify a piece of information. She'd been her old self entirely once more. It'd been a long while since she'd felt this way. Since she'd felt like who she really was.

The woman leaving the Pitt Street HQ radiated none of the self-doubt or resentment she'd fallen prey to these last few months. Graham exited onto the street, nudging past her wordlessly to clamber sourly into the car. Jackson followed shortly after. Moving to stand to Kathy's right, he lit one of his liquorice-wrapped roll-ups and blew the smoke from the side of his mouth as he spoke.

"Good job today, McGuire."

Kathy bobbed her head at his hand.

"Can I have one of those, sir?"

Jackson's brow furrowed, but he fished his tobacco tin and rolled her a slim cigarette.

Handing it to her, he asked, "Taking up new habits?"

"Returning to old ones, for a while at least."

They smoked in silence for five minutes as Graham waited in the car.

Despite the quiet there was something in the simple act of sharing the time smoking together that lent the minutes they spent on the cold street an amiability that their relationship hadn't enjoyed to date, despite the hundreds of hours they'd spent working together. For the first time, he felt like a comrade to her.

Jackson ended the moment. Flicking his cigarette end to spin into a nearby drain, Jackson resumed his customary stoicism.

"Let's get a move on, McGuire."

***

Late evening had fallen by the time they returned to Edinburgh. The journey home had been mercifully silent. Even Graham had suppressed his normally incessant chatting. Something had shifted in the dynamic between them, they all sensed it, but none wished to confront or even acknowledge it just yet.

Joining a queue of traffic at Barnton, Jackson muttered something about traffic being heavy for the time of night as he surveyed a long line of vehicles leading along Queensferry Road past Drum Brae. Kathy couldn't care less at that moment. She'd had her first little victory in a very long while. She intended to move forward in the same manner. Get on top of things at work, support Bobby more and find time for the kids. Where only insurmountable obstacles and demands had stood, she now saw a clear path and opportunities to build on her success.

Kathy braced herself against the door frame as Jackson swung the car out of the lane they were queued in. "I'll go around the back way," he announced, steering the car into the straight-ahead lane over towards Cramond. Finding that Barnton Grove was filling with detoured cars, Jackson continued straight on towards Cramond proper.

After a short while, they emerged out into Granton. It was a pain in the rear taking a long detour, but experience told them that with an incident on Queensferry Road, even such a circuitous route would get them back to Fettes more quickly than the direct one.

Graham banged heavily on the dashboard, startling both Jackson and Kathy.

"Stop! Pull in, Steve," he roared at Jackson.

Unquestioningly, Jackson screeched into the side of the road.

Scanning around to locate the cause for Graham's warning, Kathy's eyes fixed on a couple near the entrance to some rundown flats. The man, clad in bright orange T, was shoving roughly at his female companion. A particularly brutal push felled the woman. Staggering unsurely to her feet, she composed herself and threw a punch at her assailant.

A knife flashed in his hand. A lightning fast slash left a bright red line across her right cheek.

Moving faster than Kathy had thought him capable, Graham left the car, followed immediately by Jackson who shouted over his shoulder for Kathy to call it in.

Tugging hard at the door handle, Kathy swore loudly as the locking mechanism prevented her from opening the door from inside. Clambering through the gap in the front seats, Kathy cursed police vehicles. Grabbing at the radio transmitter, she spared a glance at her colleagues. Jackson tore across the precinct towards the flats. Kathy had never suspected the big sergeant could move so swiftly. Graham had almost reached the couple, only to watch the man force his victim through the entrance at knife point.

"Backup required urgently," Kathy spoke firmly into the transmitter. Relaying the address to the dispatcher, she left the radio handset on the passenger seat and took off after her colleagues.

By the time Kathy reached the heavy door to the flats, Jackson had already vanished inside, on the coattails of Graham. Reassured by the approaching noise of a siren, Kathy followed after.

Scanning around the entrance, Kathy found all the apartment doors shut tightly. A loud cry from the next floor up sent her hurrying to join her colleagues.

One tattered apartment door lay open on the first landing.

Another cry from a male voice sent her barrelling into the apartment.

Dimly lit, the small apartment was stifling. Hot air seemed to pull at Kathy as she sped inside. The smell of cannabis plants, lots of them, permeated the place.

Rounding the end of the hallway, Kathy entered the living room to find three men attacking her colleagues and a fourth – the guy they'd followed from outside – with his wicked-looking army knife against the girl's throat, its razor edge pressing her against the wall.

Graham was atop a guy in a Hibs top in his twenties. Knee pressed into the younger man's chest, the veteran DC held him pinned down with his back to the floor. Hands on each of the man's wrists, Graham fought to keep the prone man from slashing at him with a steak knife.

Jackson had engaged two of the men. With the larger of the two in a choke hold, Jackson clung to his man, rotating him around the room in front of him, shielding himself from the third man who wielded a Stanley blade. Eyes narrowing, Kathy assessed the room, quickly deciding where the greatest need was.

Protocol dictated that she assists the girl first. Her gut screamed at her to aid Jackson.

Meeting his eyes briefly, an unspoken understanding passed between them. Kathy turned to the man threatening the girl. Unaware or simply unconcerned by her presence, he was entirely focused on his victim.

"You fackin' grassing cow," he snarled at her.

She turned her face from him, showing him her cheek. Defiant disdain burned from her eyes and expression.

Stood behind and to the side of the couple, Kathy felt sure that he had fixed all of his awareness on the girl. With untapped strength and ferocious speed, she slammed herself into his side. Fortune blessed her and his face slammed hard against the concrete wall. The large knife, smooth on one edge and jagged on the other, dropped from his grasp as he slid, face down, onto the floor. Kathy swept it under the sofa with a foot, then brought as much of her weight down onto the back of his head via her heel.

A deep crunch at the moment of impact brought a bitter smile to Kathy's lips. The girl took a moment to spit on his unconscious form, locked determined eyes with Kathy, then fled from the apartment.

The downed man and the girl forgotten, Kathy whipped around to assess the room. Graham was struggling to maintain his hold on the younger man. Sweat ran in torrents down his face; his hair looked damp with it. His arms shook with the effort.

Jackson's shield was fading fast. The chokehold had done its job, seemingly more quickly than Jackson had planned on and the large man fell on to the floor in a deep oblivion.

The man with the Stanley blade did not hesitate. Lunging forward, he slashed at Steve Jackson, who retreated quickly but left the encounter with a long crimson slash along his right shoulder. Instinct drove Kathy. Again she ran and again she slammed a man from behind. Intending to drive her shoulder into the small of his back with all the force she could summon, Kathy tucked her arms in tight, her chin into her chest and averted her eyes at the moment of intended impact.

This one heard her coming. Stepping to the left, he turned his body side on, easily avoiding her charge. Kathy barrelled past, but covered only a few paces. An iron grip closed on the back of her neck and the floor changed places with the ceiling.

Thrown backwards, she watched him sneer as she fell at pace. A moment later, his elbow slammed into her nose. Through blood and tears and snot, she watched helplessly as he crouched to slash at her neck. Jackson stepped forward, delivering a heavy front kick into the side of her attacker's face. The man's neck lurched sharply to an angle it was never intended to achieve. Falling limp, the blade-merchant's eyes searched Kathy's. Asher vison cleared she watched his puzzlement as he tried to rise to his feet only to jerk violently back onto his side. Twice more he attempted to rise, once to his feet, the next to his knees. Both times his body betrayed him. Something vital was broken in the man.

Jackson held her face in both of his hands. "Kathy. You with me?" he asked calmly.

Spitting a glob of gunge from her throat, she gasped deeply. "Yes. . . Graham?" She craned her neck around then rolled around and up onto her knees.

The world lost all colour. . . except for red and Hibs-green.

Graham was on his back, his throat cut around so deeply that Kathy could see the gristly-wet shine of his larynx. His attacker wore a horrified expression, his eyes round in apparent disbelief at what he had done. A primal, animal noise came from Jackson an instant before he strode past Kathy, knocking her onto her side with his passing.

Upside-down, she watched Jackson pin the Hibee to the floor and begin raining heavy blows down onto his face. The force of each impact was such that the killer's legs jerked violently each time Jackson struck.

Finding that she cared little for the killer's rights or his welfare, Kathy forced herself up onto her feet on shaky legs. Removing her top, she tore a neat strip, severing the right arm at the seam.

Approaching Graham, Kathy watched in horror as a spurt of dark blood spouted from both sides of his neck. She could tell from the ebb of the blood, and the lack of volume, that his heart was already weakening. So much blood spread throughout the grubby carpet. He couldn't have had much left to give.

Wrapping the fabric around Graham's neck, Kathy ignored the voice inside telling her coldly that it was already too late. She tied the macabre scarf tightly. With wide eyes, Graham searched her face, pleading. He tried to speak. A blood bubble popped from his wound. Kathy held his face and kissed his forehead.

"You'll be fine, Craig. You'll be just fine," she whispered.

Removing the other sleeve, Kathy reinforced the first. It was pointless. No more blood flowed. Graham was dead.

With glassy eyes he lay back, staring at the ceiling. Despair invited Kathy to indulge it at that moment. She ignored its call and reached out to close Graham's. . . Craig's eyes.

Awareness of the room rushed back in, assaulting her shrill senses. Wet, heavy hands battered relentlessly at meat and bone. Jackson was simply gone. Lost in his wrath, he continued to drive his battered fists into the killer's unmoving face. Unwilling or unable, Kathy could not find the will to intervene.

A snarl and a spit from the corner of the room pulled her from the moment. The big guy in lurid orange, the one whose face she'd smashed against the wall, was on his feet again. Blade in hand, he fixed his eyes on Jackson and tore across the room.

Intent on his man, Jackson was unaware of the danger.

"Jackson!"

Before she heard her own voice, before she knew that she was moving, Kathy had placed herself in between the charging man and her sergeant. Her peripheral vision caught movement, Jackson's head whipping around. His face morphed from rage to fear in a micro-second.

Kathy felt cold steel enter her abdomen and scrape her hip bone. The big man pulled her close and shoved another few inches of the blade into her body. Compounding the injury, he dragged the blade out with an upward force, tearing the flesh with the serrated edge of the blade. Ragged agony swallowed Kathy.

As the last part of the blade withdrew, he threw Kathy behind him with rough disdain to resume his charge at Jackson.

Pain became her entire existence. With all of Kathy's strength she strove to endure. To remain conscious. As the world retreated, she watched Jackson and the man connect in a heavy collision. Kathy's eyes rolled into blackness.

Now...

17

Tequila Mockingbird Blog Kill 18

Gary McCabeis dead. Few will miss a man like Gary, likely no-one will. Gary did not die peacefully or quickly, he did not deserve to. Gary died in pain, a lot of it, issued at my hand over many hours. I could've spent days taking Gary McCabe apart and wouldn't have come close to the agonies he spent years eagerly inflicting on his wife.

Gary was a very physical abuser. Lacking the mental prowess needed to truly intimidate and manipulate, he preferred to break bones, bruise flesh and open wounds in his wife's skin.

Irene McCabe was stitched and stapled and cast in plaster many times over the years. Each time, she made excuses for him, to herself, to the police. She lied for the abuser. She convinced herself that she had earned her scars.

Irene is free now and completely blameless in her husband's death. I broke three of the bones in his right hand. I shattered his right femur. I stabbed his kidney, severed his spinal cord and pulled three of his teeth. Big ones.

Molars.

Some of this Gary did not feel, due to my severing of his spinal cord, but my goodness did he suffer mentally as I picked apart his notion of himself as all powerful; in control. . . Master of his house and everyone in it.

Irene played no role in his death. I acted alone.

I know these things about Gary McCabe. I punished Gary McCabe, because I watched him for a long time. I saw how he controlled and victimised those he should have loved and cherished.

Gary will never harm Irene, or anyone else again.

Press In,

Tequila

"Please welcome author of the *Vampire Junior High* books, Alice Connolly." The head teacher smiles into the wings, beckoning me onto the stage. Standing there, absent any disguising makeup or wig, naked of any clothes save my own, I feel incredibly vulnerable.

Who could imagine feeling so alien simply due to being oneself for a few hours?

Shoving my innate fear of being in front of so many eyes aside, I remind myself that the assembly hall full of school children needs moments like this, as do I and straighten my back whilst arranging an expression of warmth which I genuinely feel, but am having trouble convincing my facial muscles of.

The teacher at the piano at the foot of the stage plays the opening theme to the movie of *Vampire Junior High: Vein Glorious* and those assembled welcome me with applause, bringing a blush to my cheeks as I take my place at the mic. Pushing the rising panic down, I focus on the faces in the front row. The smallest children, the P1s, sit cross-legged and cute, eyes wide, smiles beaming up at me. Their innocent expectation of who and what I am, the fearless author of books that carry them to other worlds, is evident. My nerves promptly vanish and the mask of that person slips easily into place.

"Good morning, boys and girls." I make my voice soft, hoping to dampen the electric feel of the room.

The children respond by leaning in intently.

"Thank you so much for such a lovely welcome to your school." I lock eyes with a series of the younger kids, talking to them directly, one at a time. "You look wonderful today," I tell them, meaning it.

They're dressed in an endless myriad of costumes and hold replica items from my movies. It's quite something to see children invested so in characters and stories I created.

"Your costumes are fantastic. Thank you so much."

My publisher, David, stands off in the wings alongside my literary agent, Jessica. They're beaming almost as much as the kids are, but for very different reasons. These events are all well and fine, from their perspective, more readers mean more money. They're not bad people, they're just doing their job of increasing exposure and improving revenue. Generally, I try to ignore the machine my books have become and focus on the reach I've attained. More children reading; more of them engaging in books. It's quite something, but you can't have that engagement without the business to drive it.

I bring my focus back onto the kids in front of me. As I'm about to resume, something tugs at my subconscious. Today's agenda is intended to be a simple speech about creativity and encouraging the kids to do what they love in life, followed by a few anecdotes about writing their favourite characters. Suddenly, I don't feel like doing this anymore.

Taking the mic in my hand, I leave the stage, speaking as I descend the stairs.

"If it's okay with your teachers, I'd like to do something a little more fun with you today, kids."

I glance around at the nearest teachers and the head teacher who are nodding their agreement enthusiastically. Relaxing fully for the first time, I come down to my haunches in front of the younger kids in the front row.

"I'd like you to organise yourselves, with your teachers' help, into your classes." A slight shuffle waves through the room as the kids start to rise. "Not so fast, kids!"

They resettle quickly, their teachers grin at their eagerness.

"Once you're in your class groups, I'd like you to pick a character, or a scene, or a chapter from your favourite book from my series." I move my eyes over their faces, smiling at them. "Now, I don't want any arguing," I tell them playfully. "I'd like you to reach an agreement on which aspect you'll focus on and then take that character or moment from the books or films and change the story to what you *would* have liked to have seen happen instead, or create a scene set afterwards."

A ripple of excitement pervades the room. Teachers lean in, shushing their charges. "You can do anything with your stories. Take the characters or plots anywhere you like. Be creative, be dangerous, and while you discuss, I'll be moving throughout the hall, listening in. Holy Family Primary, I can't wait to hear where our imaginations take us today."

It takes the teachers ten minutes to organise the groups of children into circles and huddles of busy activity. Some have fetched poster paper and are plotting out scenes and drawing incidents they've created. Others have lined or blank paper spread out before them and are lost in their own heads, scribbling down adventures. A group of P4s are animatedly acting out their ideas. The older kids have split themselves into smaller groups, based not on friendships, but rather on skills. The artist sketches rough outlines, the writers jot down structure, the physical kids play act their ideas. They take the characters and stories to places I never could. It's startling and it is humbling. Children have always elicited the warmest emotions in me.

Looking around the hall my heart suddenly lurches in my chest. This. . . this is the power of books. Almost unseen, I move amongst them, soaking up their enthusiasm, thriving on the energy and creativity these young people possess and share guilelessly.

It may well be the happiest moment of my entire life.

My afternoon races by me in a series of revelations, entertainments and what are quite simply the most fulfilling moments I've spent in the company of other people. Thanking the children and teachers and promising to visit them again soon, I leave the school with a light step and happy heart. Despite the elation I'm feeling, I make it perhaps one mile from the school building on the back of my Ducati when my 'real self' slides coldly back over me. For the first time in as long as I recall, I feel a little regret at the change in my frame of mind.

By late evening I'm sat in the rear section of an internet café I use on rotation with twelve others in the city, accessing the dark web from my white phone.

As soon as I switch the phone on, the screen lights up and the handset vibrates with a stream of notifications from the blog and Twitter feeds.

The increase in traffic and followers, which began as I was prepping for the McCabe kill, has grown exponentially in the last thirty hours or so. The blog now carries three hundred thousand followers. My Twitter profile has over one million. From as many countries as I can name, they've begun tracking my progress, retweeting me, sharing my blog entries. Something vital has shifted and I'm clueless as to what. That can be remedied though.

Sifting and backtracking through the river of comments and shares, I make my way doggedly along the digital trail.

The sheer number of Tweets and comments is staggering. Their tone is overwhelmingly supportive.

@MaggieMoo: We love you Tequila.

@Squidgytail: Those bastards deserve everything you've done and more.

@PinkEdition: We want to interview you for our piece on 21st century feminism.

@MightyGirlz: Finally, a feminist warrior.

@JohnnyT: Slag.

@JeanniePeenie: She is a cold blooded psychotic serial killer who has found a justifiable reason to murder. If it wasn't this there would be another excuse.

Scanning and backtracking I read one in fifty Tweets addressed to my profile. The comments on my blog draw me more strongly.

Women of all ages from a seemingly never-ending series of races and backgrounds, social status and nationality have contacted me, commenting on my entries. Some voice messages of support for my actions but far too many take the opportunity to relay their own experiences with an abusive partner. After reading six women's stories, I vow to read no more, fearful that I'll shatter my detachment and collapse under the weight of their trust and what they are enduring. Worse, that I indulge the killer in me to a degree I can ill-afford.

Forensically, I work my way through a timeline of events, coming at last to the entry that tipped the avalanche.

A woman from a domestic violence support charity quoted my tweet containing the McKenna killing to Beyhanna, who not only retweeted it to her eighty million Twitter followers, but also published a long, heart-wrenching essay detailing her own experiences with an abusive partner. Years of meticulous planning and killing, journaling each of them as a show of support for those still under threat from an abuser, and it's a tweet and blog from a singer that breaks the dam. It seems that it's my day to connect with people.

I lean back into the plastic chair, suddenly very aware I'm in a public place. Looking around the café, I confirm that none of the nerds, business people or gamers present care about me in the least. Wearing a dark wig, with a severe chopped fringe, even the biggest Vampire Junior High fan would walk straight past me.

The intense feeling of eyes on me I experienced earlier in the day returns but magnified many thousands of times. I force myself through my breathing exercises. Calming, I remind myself that this was always the goal. That I'm protected, anonymous as can be behind layer upon layer of algorithm and code and the dark web. Seb taught me well. His tech guy has ensured that anyone trying to trace my online signature will simply be bounced around a hundred thousand dead ends. My Twitter account and blog, whilst publicly visible, are linked only to email accounts via the dark web and untraceable to Alice Connolly. If the companies close the accounts down, as is a definite possibility, I'll simply begin again and repeat over and over. My white phone is a pay as you go, unconnected to anyone.

Feeling my heart begin to slow to normal, I resist the urge to check around the café once again and resume my research.

Beyhanna's blog stops short of condoning my violence against abusers, but only just. She asks some surprisingly insightful questions showing a perceptiveness and empathy I hadn't thought her capable of, judging by her public image.

Has our casual acceptance of violence against women culminated in the need for a killer who redresses these injustices?

Is Tequila a necessary evil?

I nod along as I read the blog for a third time. She includes a link to my own blog in her signature. I click back to my blog's dashboard and watch the follower count tick by for a few moments as more people sign up to it. I silence the notifications in the setting menu. My phone will have no charge remaining and will have vibrated a hole in the table if I don't. Checking my Twitter profile, I find my followers at almost two million. A perfunctory scan through the list finds that most of them are women or news agencies.

As I'm reading through the list, a tweet pops through that draws my eye:

@PoliceScotlandDIMcGuire: @TequilaMockingbird. Stop what you are doing, now.

Excitement races through me. I perform a quick mental check designed to ensure that I'm not acting solely on impulse therefore self-sabotaging. With a nod of confirmation I send my reply:

@TequilaMockingbird: @PoliceScotlandDIMcGuire. *Kill 18 Violent, Body-shamer and Wife beater. #PressIn*

18

Police Scotland Press Conference:

DI McGuire: Thank you for coming today, ladies and gentlemen. As you are aware, Michael McKenna, of Newhaven Main Street, was murdered in his home in the early hours of Wednesday. Preliminary forensics have proven scarce but have uncovered several key factors, which I'm unable to fully share with you this morning. What I can share, however, is that, with the aid of colleagues in several UK police forces, we have determined that Mr McKenna was killed by a person or persons linked to several other cases spanning almost eight years.

Shona Collins, STV news: Are you saying that a serial killer is responsible for Mr McKenna's murder, Detective?

DI McGuire: From the MO of the killer or killers and several consistencies we've noticed when examining the physical and circumstantial evidence, we believe so, yes.

Cat Turner, BBC Scotland: Can you give us more details on what specifically has taken the enquiry in this particular direction?

DI McGuire: Not at this time. What I can say is that the person perpetrating these murders is targeting very specific individuals and has thus far not proven a danger to a broad group of people.

Hugh Kevins, Glasgow Herald: Serial killers are so rare as to be virtually unheard of in the UK, Detective. Isn't this a rather bold conclusion to arrive at, particularly in light of your inability to explain why your department have done so?

DI McGuire: You're quite correct, Mr Stevens, serial killers are not common in the UK, but if you do your research, I assure you, they arise more often than you may think. Whilst we're unable to share the specifics of our case with you for legal and strategic reasons, I can assure you and the public that we have not embarked upon this line of enquiry without very clear and very serious evidence.

Garry Crawley, The Scotsman: When you say that you have consulted with colleagues UK-wide, what exactly are we looking at here, DI McGuire? How many people do you believe have been killed by this person?

Di McGuire: We've consulted with several forces, Manchester, Liverpool, Newcastle, amongst others. We're looking at as many as sixteen murders most likely the work of the same killer. In each of the cases the victim's family has disappeared in the days around the murders.

What we'd like to do today is appeal to those family members to come forward. We know that they had very good reasons to leave their partners, and they are under no suspicion whatsoever. We just need their help and to know that they are safe. They may also have valuable evidence that they do not even realise they hold.

To the killer directly, we would like to ask that you stop the course of action you have undertaken. We know that you feel these men deserved their deaths. They did not. No matter how justified you feel in your actions, somewhere inside you know that you are simply wrong. Please do not kill any more people. Come forward and let us help you.

"Mum, squeeze in a little to your right."

James waves me over, closer to his wife Angela, who rolls her eyes at me in mock annoyance at his insistence on the perfect family photo.

"You lot look like mannequins," James complains, eliciting a ripple of laughter. He snaps off ten photos whilst we're responding to his jibe. "Perfect," he calls out, emerging from behind his camera. "You lot are a nightmare to get natural when a camera comes out."

Kathy smiles to herself, the way she always does when the similarities between James's personality and her own show as clearly as they do at that moment. Two waiters, hands full, appear and begin placing their plates out for the family. Catching Angela subconsciously rub at her temples, Kathy takes young Jack by the hand.

"C'mon, m'darlin'. Let's go look at the fish in the aquarium."

Jack leads her though the restaurant, excitedly skipping along. Kathy looks over her shoulder catching a mouthed *thank you* from her daughter-in-law. She smiles and nods in return. It's a tough shift having a lively kid like Jack around. He's a good boy, but your life isn't your own with a two-year-old at your heels. Giving Angie and James ten minutes' peace to eat their dinner is the least she can do to help out, Kathy decides.

Intending to spend ten minutes, Kathy becomes so enraptured with the precious time alone with Jack, watching his excitement at the strangely coloured fish, that she loses half an hour, caught in his infectious love of everything he experiences.

Eventually Bobby seeks them out. "Hiya, you two having fun?" he asks, smiling at Kathy who is sitting cross-legged. Jack has his rear parked on her legs for a seat.

"Grampa, come see this one. This is a blue laser fish," Jack begins.

Bobby hands Kathy her phone. The screen shows a simple one line message from Steve.

We've found another body. Looks like our killer.

"Go on, love. I'll take over."

A hand out to help haul his wife to her feet, Bobby plants a kiss on one cheek whilst cupping the other with his hand. "It's good to see you relax, Kathy," he says warmly.

"Yeah," Kathy replies. Both of them know that these are always stolen moments. They've made the best of their evening together, it's what they do, but each of them has grown accustomed to having one eye on her phone.

With Kathy in lead role on a major case, their time is never their own. Bobby's grown used to her unscheduled departures and long hours over the decades. Kathy never has. Looking up at her husband, she sees nothing but calm acceptance in his eyes. That he's become so habituated to having to make excuses for her, to fill the Kathy-shaped gap in their family unit so many times, makes her heart ache.

Returning his gesture, she cups both of his cheeks. "I love you so much, Bobby. You're such a good man."

Bobby cocks his head to the side. "This case really bothering you, love?"

Kathy shrugs. "Just making me appreciate how much support you've given me, love."

Bobby nods, accepting her words. There's no pride in his response, it's nothing to him, being the stable parent and grandparent, arranging the diary, shouldering her slack, filling the gaps. It's what he does and he's good at it.

Jack tugs at Bobby's hand. "Pay attention, Grampa," he chides.

Bobby smiles at his wife.

"You're welcome, Kathy. Now go."

As Kathy turns to leave, Bobby calls out after her, "Hey Kathy, you looked really good on the TV this morning."

Kathy smiles broadly at her husband.

"Thanks, love."

A mischievous grin on his face that reminds Kathy of the young man she fell in love with, Bobby adds, "Go catch your killer, then come home and let me appreciate my hot wife."

Jack laughs. "Hot wife," he parrots.

Kathy's eyes widen in faux annoyance. Bobby simply winks back at her.

"See you later, Bob," she promises, turning to leave.

***

Ferguson has been speaking at her for a full ten minutes now. Kathy's carefully composed facial expression makes her look as though she's listening intently. She even manages the odd nod or *uh-huh* in response. In truth she's working through the details in her mind's eye.

Ferguson has reported all the pertinent facts. *More distilled water at the scene. No forced entry. Wounds consistent in shape and pattern to those found on McKenna. Likely frozen tissue at the wounds, this time in the back of the neck and right kidney. Broken femur and fingers. Teeth removed.*

The doctor is now simply, officiously, replaying minor details that are common to almost every crime scene.

This death seems much more violent than McKenna's. The killer has still approached the murder methodically. Each wound and injury deliberate, thought out in advance, most likely, but there's a cruelty present this time that Kathy either hadn't acknowledged or wasn't present in the last murder. *Is our apparently clinical killer allowing emotion to creep into the kills, or perhaps beginning to derive pleasure from them?*

Hope bubbles. This is how serials are caught. Eventually, even the most prepared get emotional, or arrogant, or simply do not prepare so thoroughly. Eventually they seem to lose themselves in the ritual, or even reach a stage where they want to be caught.

The notion that the killer has a point to prove, that they are punishing what they see as abusive men, returns to Kathy. *A person who is doing what our killer is thinks that they are justified. More than that, they think that they're teaching the rest of us something. Surely such a person will want to be in front of an audience at some point?*

"Detective?" Ferguson's voice is tetchy. His tone suggests that he has called her name several times, unanswered.

Focusing her eyes firmly on the doctor, she apologises. "Sorry, Dr Ferguson, I zoned out a little there."

Regarding her over his glasses, Ferguson decides that she is simply overwhelmed by the information he's been relaying. He makes a little superior smirk, excusing her layman's attention span.

"Well, not to worry, I'll get a full report to you in a few hours. You can absorb the details at your own pace."

Kathy allows him to walk away without retort. In her bag, her phone vibrates insistently. She's been ignoring it for the past few hours, as is her custom when attending a crime scene.

Walking the few paces to McCabe's bedroom, Kathy takes in the scene before her. McCabe is face-down; blood has formed a puddle, soaking into the sheets near his mouth. His teeth lie on the pillow, arranged in size order, biggest to smallest. A macabre joke by the killer. The wound on his neck has bled little and shows the same discolouration of the tissue as McKenna's wounds. The kidney wound is horrific. The killer appears to have twisted the weapon inside the kidney, opening a ragged hole through which Kathy can see the dark red-brown of the savaged organ.

His broken leg is swollen and distended, as are his fingers. The doctor hasn't been able to determine whether the breaks were inflicted before or after his spinal cord was severed. If before death, then the killer took deliberate pleasure in torturing McCabe physically. If afterward, then psychological torture was the goal. Kathy shudders, unsure which scenario induces the urge to vomit that has risen in her throat.

Observing McCabe's abused body, unable to draw her eyes away, Kathy does not turn to greet Steve as he enters the room.

"Hey, Kathy, pretty severe, eh?" he offers. Kathy simply nods.

Reading from his phone, Steve leans in as he speaks to her, clearly wishing to keep the conversation private.

"Looks like young Gilmour is onto something, Kathy."

Finally, Kathy does turn to her partner, a jut of her chin his signal to continue.

"The wife, Irene, hasn't been seen for several days. I checked her medical records and she's been in and out of the A&E regularly."

Steve reads off a list of injuries Irene McCabe has had treated over several years. Kathy's phone interrupts her thoughts, vibrating for what feels like the thousandth time that day. Reaching onto her bag, Kathy switches it off without bothering to check the screen.

"Another wife-beater," Kathy says, her voice a whisper.

"Seems that way," Steve replies.

Kathy nods over at the door. "C'mon. Let's go get a coffee and talk about how to proceed."

Steve's eyebrows rise comically. "In Rutherglen? No thanks. Let's get back to Edinburgh, we can talk in the car." His comment is intended to raise a smile, but Kathy isn't in the mood.

As they move through to McCabe's hallway, Gilmour rushes into the apartment.

"Ma'am, I have something. It's important."

"With a gesture, Kathy shushes the young detective."

"Not here, Lewis. Let's get back to the station."

***

"Jeezuz, Gilmour, can't you do anything without that computer?" Steve asks tetchily.

"In this instance, sir, it is a requirement."

"Right ye are, son," Steve replies, winking at Kathy. She smiles at Steve's gentle ribbing of the junior officer but motions that he should continue setting up.

Once again, smart board in order, Gilmour brings up a website before reporting to them. From the screen, a sombre-looking site designed with clean lines in predominantly black and green, shines down at them. The legend 'Tequila Mockingbird' sits atop the home page. Three tabs are stationed directly beneath:

About. Archives. Contact Tequila.

"A friend of mine texted me a link to this earlier today. Until recently the site, which is mainly a blog, had gone fairly unnoticed. With only a hundred or so followers, the blog and the linked Twitter profile, have been in existence for around two years. During that time, few people have read the posts. Most of those who have haven't bothered to comment on or report the content.

From those who've engaged with the blog or the Twitter feed, it's clear that they've assumed that it's a parody blog, or perhaps a series of fiction instalments from a writer attempting to draw attention in for a book perhaps."

Gilmour swallows hard, clearly steeling himself.

"In the last eighteen hours or so, the number of people following this account and its Twitter feed has reached the millions. As far as I can ascertain, this upsurge in interaction and discovery has been the result of a retweet and blog essay about the site by the singer Beyhanna."

Steve sits back into his chair. Clearly unimpressed by Gilmour's report, he manages to stay silent, but his face shows scorn.

Gilmour ignores Steve's reaction, focusing on Kathy who has her full attention on him.

"Tequila's blogs not only detail a series of murders, which most readers believed fictional, but also explain her motives for killing the men."

With a gesture, Gilmour brings up a blog entry detailing McKenna's murder.

Open-mouthed, Kathy and Steve read through her account of the man's brutal death. Tequila's blog contains details only the killer could have included.

"God," Kathy utters. "Is this visible to the public?"

Face ashen, Gilmour confirms that it is. "Anyone who wishes to read these blogs can, ma'am."

Kathy suddenly recalls her annoyingly busy phone, switched off and forgotten in her bag.

Steve is now on his feet. "Well, that's it, then. We trace the blog and Twitter user and we have her."

Gilmour manages to keep a sympathetic look from his eyes in response to the naivety of his superior. "I'm afraid not, sir. The accounts have been setup using the dark web. The account holder is at present untraceable to our techs."

"The dark what?" Steve asks looking around at Kathy to find her as clueless as himself.

"It's a general term used by people with little knowledge of computer communication." he gestures at Kathy and Steve, "to refer to a method of accessing the internet that leaves the user anonymous."

"Right," Steve accuses angrily. "Well, that's fuckin' handy, isn't it?"

Uncertain how to respond, Gilmour remains silent.

"Can't the sites just remove her access to them? Surely a killer detailing how she's murdered people violates their user agreement?"

"They absolutely can, sir, but. . ."

Steve rounds on the junior officer. "But nothing, Gilmour. Contact Word Press and Twitter UK and get those posts removed. If we can't trace her, we can sure as hell take her access away."

Kathy watches the exchange without interjecting.

Gilmour is caught between taking a direct order and expressing his opinion on how to proceed. The kid digs in and stands to confront Steve, who is growing angrier by the second.

"Sir, with all due respect, I believe that removing the blog and Twitter feed would not only be a futile gesture, but would also remove a potentially invaluable resource for our investigation."

Watching the two men squared up to each other, Kathy leans back onto her desk. Experience has taught her that these things are better left played out and then mopped up once the players have run out of steam.

Steve surprises her by swallowing his anger, at least a little and backing away from the young constable. Taking a seated posture that is anything but relaxed, Steve finally asks, "Go on then, Gilmour. Explain to me why I should let a serial killer promote, boast and incite using this blog?"

To his credit, Gilmour doesn't hesitate. He even manages to maintain his respectful tone.

"Sir, if we remove the blog and the Twitter profile, she will simply begin another anew. It's ridiculously easy to do. With the number of followers she has and the growing buzz around the blog, she could set up a new account every day and her followers would not only find each new account as it arises, but grow in number simply because of the challenge the blog-hopping would represent. We would empower and amplify her posts."

Waiting for Steve to challenge him, Gilmour gives the sergeant a few seconds' silence in which to vent. Looking emboldened, Gilmour picks up the thread without interjection from Kathy or Steve.

"Nobody has ever done anything like this before, sir. This will be huge, it already is. The user interaction has already gone ballistic on the blog. Her Twitter profile has had more retweets and comments than almost any other profile today. There's a power in that, but it's not all in her favour."

Kathy takes a brief pause in Gilmour's monologue to glance over at Steve. He's still angry, but is visibly warming to what Gilmour is proposing.

"We have a serial killer and a female one at that. That's rare enough in itself, but that she is willing to communicate her motivation, her intentions and her methods to us, well, it's quite something."

"She's willing to communicate alright. She's goading us, Gilmour. . ."

"No, sir," Gilmour interrupts angrily. "She is not. She is explaining herself. She's giving us a glut of evidence." Gilmour is visibly shaking. "Jack the Ripper sent notes to the Whitechapel detectives to mock and goad them, but this isn't the same at all. She has an agenda. She wants to frighten people, mainly abusive men, but she's not interested in mocking. She's serious. She thinks that she is a force for good."

Kathy nods along at his words. "He's right, Steve. She thinks that she's saving these women."

"Yes!" Gilmour leaps on the encouragement. "She doesn't care that we're reading these posts. They're not for us. They're a warning to abusers and. . ." Gilmour's eyes flick to Steve. He knows the sergeant won't like his next words. "And they're a symbol of hope for abused spouses. That is what she intends to be."

"She's a bloody murderer, son. Not some romantic avenger."

"I agree, sir, but whether she means to or not, whether she cares or not, by writing these blogs she's giving us an insight into her actions that no killer ever has before whilst still active. She's giving us what we need to anticipate and perhaps, predict her."

The corner of Steve's mouth turns up a minute amount, somewhere between a smile and a sneer. "You've some balls on you, kid."

Gilmour manages to look contrite. "Sir."

Kathy finally stands, positioning herself deliberately at Gilmour's side.

"What do you suggest, Lewis?"

"Leave the blog up, use it. Wait until she gets arrogant. With the interaction she's receiving she will respond in some way." Abruptly Gilmour breaks into a wide-eyed grin. "We should contact her directly. Try to get a dialogue going."

Instantly Steve is on his feet again, glaring at Gilmour. "Absolutely not."

Even as the words leave his mouth, his eyes move to Kathy's face. One look at his long-term partner confirms that he's already lost this argument.

"Set me a Twitter profile up, Lewis. Let's see what we can make happen."

Then...

19

I came around to the soundtrack of wet thumps and begging cries. My eyes wouldn't open. Tilting my head to better hear, I searched the room with my ears.

"I'm sorry, Darren." Thump.

"Darren, the baby." Thump.

Thump. Thump. Thump.

As the room eventually grew silent, my eyes finally did as I bid them and showed me the broken world around us. Darren stood over the prone body of my little sister, his back and chest heaving with effort. Nicole's eyes were open, but they were blank. She'd taken herself elsewhere, somewhere the horror this moment had become couldn't reach her. To escape our father's violence, she'd done this exact same thing as a child. It was how she'd survived him.

Laid there, eyes glazed, folded protectively around her barely-showing bump, Nicole bled from a cut to her eye, her forearm and from between her legs. Darren muttered something inaudible to me between rasping breaths.

An image of Nicole as a baby danced before my mind's-eye. She was a beautiful child, a good baby, quiet and content. She became a precocious teen and a formidable young woman. Always, I felt a parent to her rather than her sister. At times a parent was what I was to her. *So alike*, that's what they always said of us but I never felt that way, I always felt responsible for her. I still did.

In a sickening explosion of violence, he stomped on her lower back. In response, I hauled myself dizzily to my feet and ran at him. Even with all the speed I could muster and my entire body weight; even with him stood, lost in his own red fury, unaware of my approach; even with the rage of a lifetime to power my charge I barely managed to knock him to the ground.

Despite being unable to control my momentum, I recovered more quickly than he did, bringing my foot down with force onto his nose. He screamed like the weakling he was as the bone split under my heel. I felt some satisfaction at his pain.

I grabbed a heavy lamp from the table on my right and brought it crashing down onto his face. Rather than cow him, the double blow, the viciousness of my assault, enraged and empowered Darren, gifting him an adrenaline flood that brought him surging to his feet. Before I'd had the opportunity to take even a half-step away from his clutching hands, he had me by the throat in a steel cable grip.

Using all of his considerable strength and weight, he forced me onto my back and placed a thick knee across my neck and jaw. When he pressed down the world disappeared into two pinpoint holes at the centre of darkness.

As my mind slipped away again, he lifted the pressure. I gasped in a hoarse broken breath and my eyes let the light back in again. The very last thing I saw was his fists pummelling my face as I lay helpless. My last thoughts were with my sister.

***

With great effort, Nicole shoved at the carpet with both hands, bringing herself to her knees. Deepest pain, ancient and primal, gouged her insides at the effort. Nicole internalised the pain and lifted her head.

Darren was on his knees, one leg either side of Alice's abdomen, raining blows relentlessly into her face and chest. Lost in his fury, he had pummelled his fists bloody. Alice's blood mingled and splashed with his own in the violence of the moment.

Placing one foot under her, Nicole almost collapsed as a violent cramp moved mercilessly down through her body. Waiting for it to pass, she finally stood on uncertain legs. Something was running down her thighs and onto her shins to pool at her feet.

She screamed internally, demanding that her mind not allow itself to focus on the little life leaving her body. Compelling herself to look at her sister's brutalised face, Nicole stoked her anger, converting it to mental will and physical strength.

Memories of their father rose, but reinforced her determination to act rather than sapped her of it. On wet feet, she padded through to the kitchen, unnoticed by the monster in her living room. A wave of nausea and despair almost brought her low. A hand on a kitchen counter became her anchor to her resolve. Closing her other hand around the grip of a long knife in the block, Nicole felt its weight as a reassurance.

The fleshy thumps coming from the next room had begun to slow as the monster tired. Nicole's eyes narrowed and fixed on the beast in her home. His back to her, his solid blows had become exhausted slaps. He remained unaware of her approach. An instant before the blade kissed the skin of his neck, Darren sensed her. He snapped his head upwards to look up at her. Despite the fatigue in his muscles, his eyes still blazed with intense abandon. Calmly, Nicole slid the knife into his neck and pulled it towards herself, slicing three inches of skin open. Blood fountained from the open gash, ebbed and then spouted once again in rhythm with his heart. Nicole stood, mannequin-like, idly wondering how she would get the stains from the carpet and curtains.

Darren died angrily and quickly, much quicker than he deserved. Falling onto his face beside Alice's body, this man who had made himself the centre of her existence became less than nothing, meaningless, in Nicole's mind. A wind seemed to stir the room, returning Nicole to the horror her life had become.

Falling to her knees, Nicole searched her sister's broken and bloodied face. No breath escaped her lips, her still-open eyes puffy, partly closed over and lifeless. She wiped blood and tissue from Alice's cheeks, shook her head roughly. A wet crimson bubble grew and popped at her sister's lifeless lips. A last escape of air from her lungs.

Alice was gone.

The thought was too much.

Alice. Alice. Alice.

On her knees, Nicole leaned back, her shoulders coming to meet her heels. A low, animal moan escaped without volition. Something vital broke free from her spirit and departed without a backward glance. Soon after, her body contributed to the loss. A thick stream of tissue formed a lump at Nicole's groin. Removing her underwear, she retrieved and cradled her unborn infant in the palm of her right hand. Three inches long, fully formed. Little eyes closed, asleep forever, Nicole's child slumbered in her hand. A twitch from a tiny arm sent Nicole's mind elsewhere.

***

Images flickered through my mind. Alice and I as children. Dad standing over me, fists raised. Alice intervening. Alice taking the beating meant for me.

Our mother, crumpled in the corner of the room, her bruised eyes averted, convincing herself she wasn't present. Useless. Alice, blood and bruises, comforting her, comforting me. Alice telling Social Services, finally freeing us from him.

Alice coaching me for exams at school, at university. Alice working straight out of school and into the bank, providing, supporting Mum and I, placing her own ambitions, her dreams aside for our sakes.

Mum dead; a blend of grief and relief bringing us low. Alice pulling us both from the depression of being orphaned, bringing us back into the light.

Alice. Alice. Alice.

How do I function without her?

How can I be this coward? How can I endure as this weakling who allowed this to happen to us?

The mother with her tiny baby's corpse in her hand?

I cannot tolerate this life, not one moment longer.

I need Alice.

I sent my conscious self willingly into the oblivion I'd retreated to since I was a young child. Feeling the darkness enclose warmly around me, I didn't bother to say goodbye to reality. I had no use for a reality so cruel and filled with horrors. I did not wish to exist as Nicole any longer.

Alice.

Alice. The strong one. Alice the capable, inspirational woman I could never have been. Alice was required for a world like this one.

Alice…lice……………………………………………
…………………………………………………………
…………………………………………………………
…………………………………………………………
…………………………………………………………
………………………………………………………

***

Dead matter falling forgotten from my hand, I stood. Coldly, pragmatically, I observed the dead body of my sister before me then flicked my eyes away to survey the room, formulating a course of action. I picked out a path for survival from the debris of my former life. With purpose I moved. Leaving the living room behind, I ascended the staircase to Nicole's bedroom. A long mirror met me as I entered. For several seconds, I recall standing observing myself in her mirror, making mental adjustments to my appearance which I judged needed to be made so that I might once again feel like myself. They could wait, I decided. I'd take care of what I could now and worry about the finer details later.

I showered, scrubbing hard at my skin, shedding all deadness from it. The blood of four people ran and pooled to spin down the drain as I scrubbed at my scalp. With little haste, I dried my hair, arranging it into my customary ponytail with one loose stream of hair framing my face. I'd do something about the colour later.

Once dressed in clothes from my suitcase, I retrieved my handbag from the living room, paying little heed to the mess present. Wishing to leave nothing to chance, I confirmed the presence of my passport, return ticket to San Francisco, my diary, including Seb's details and some ready cash. Running my fingers across my name on the passport, *Alice Kinney,* I felt my resolve tighten once again.

Alice.

Following a search through the kitchen cupboards, I returned to the living room. Moving throughout the room, I sprayed and splashed curtains, the sofa, a section of the carpet, even the bodies of Darren and my sister, with the lighter fuel I'd found.

Hesitating over the finger-sized body of Nicole's child, I felt a tug from somewhere in the deepest part of my consciousness. My legs began to tremble.

Violently, I willed silence from that part of my former self, banishing her weakness. Without emotion, I poured the remainder of the lighter fluid over the child.

A barrier slid shut inside my mind, closing it forever. Fetching and lighting a house candle, I said no words of comfort or grief. I simply threw the lit candle onto Darren's back where it took the accelerant instantly, sending an orange-blue flamelicking and darting throughout the living room to cleanse it.

My bag over my shoulder, I exited the growing inferno. Without regret, I left Nicole and her life behind. Consumed by orange blaze and my own will, she was gone forever.

20

Bobby was there with Kathy once again. Bobby and Jackson, Jackson and Bobby. Each of them took shifts, sitting by her side, chiding, blessing and cursing her, commanding her to be strong. Both of them had cried. Several times. Jackson read to her at times. Sometimes he told her of his life, details he never shared before with Kathy: all of his losses, his hopes for the future, his fears.

Awareness came to Kathyin shifts. She didn't know how long she'd been in the hospital bed. When Kathy woke, it always seemed to be night. Bobby or Jackson, one was by the bedside. She was never alone. Not once.

Kathy tried to swallow and found only rawness where moisture should be.

In response to a weak noise, Bobby rose to his feet, taking her hand. When she opened her eyes again, it was daytime. The sun shone behind her husband's face. He looked so tired.

"Kathy, oh my darlin'."

His voice was almost as weak as Kathy's. Something in his eyes told her that he'd doubted she would wake.

Kathy pointed at a water jug to her right. With careful hands, Bobby propped his wife up, her back against a pillow. The bed rose mechanically. Deep, intrusive pain stabbed at Kathy's midriff. Bobby pressed the glass against her chin, popping a straw into her mouth so that she might drink.

"Not too much at once, Kathy," he warned.

For a wonder, she listened to his advice. The water felt cool, healing and intrusive. Kathy turned her head from the straw. Bobby searched her eyes, assessing exactly who had woken up to him.

Kathy tried an experimental cough and almost cried at the pain in her throat. Swallowing carefully, she attempted a whisper this time.

"How long?"

"Two days, love. You had a ruptured kidney, it was carved apart by the knife."

Kathy let out a weak laugh. "Thought I'd been here for weeks."

Abruptly her eyes widened. "How's Steve? I thought he'd been here. . .?"

Bobby placed a hand gently onto her shoulder, suggesting that she not move lest she tear open something vital.

"Steve is fine, Kathy. A few bruises, a cut or two. He was here, lots of times." Bobby's slight grin told her that her husband liked Jackson. "He came as often as he could, even helped out with the kids so that I could do the shopping, visit you. . . He's been great, really."

Kathy's mind raced, trying to reconcile Bobby's new best pal with the gruff, isolated man she'd worked under for years. Sensing her confusion, Bobby added, "I think he had a big shock," he nodded down at her abdomen, "with what happened to you, Kathy. He's been desperately worried."

"Jackson?" she asked, unable to hide her disbelief.

Bobby laughed softly. "Yes, Jackson."

"Should've got stabbed years ago then," Kathy tried a laugh, but a sharp pain in her side stole it from the room.

Regarding her husband's tired face, she felt the familiar guilt return.

"Are we alright, Bobby?"

Bobby's eyebrows raised high on his forehead.

"You're pretty far from alright, Kathy McGuire."

"You know what I mean."

Bobby's faux indignation vanished.

"Yeah. We're alright, but things need to change, Kathy. We can't continue as we have."

Kathy nodded along.

She'd expected at some point that she'd be forced to choose between a career she loved and the needs of her family. In truth, she'd expected it to have arisen years before.

As much as she would despair leaving her career, there was simply no contest. Bobby and the kids had to come first.

"I know. I'll recover, wrap up some loose work I have on my desk and move on, Bobby."

Kathy's face turned from her husband. She loved him, she was devoted to her family, but the loss of her career was a huge price to pay for their happiness.

Bobby's warm hand settled on one of her own.

"I don't want that at all, Kathy," he said.

Turning her gaze back to him, she narrowed her eyes. A questioning gesture.

Hope flared in her.

"I want you to keep working hard at your career, Kathy. You're good at it. Hell, you're great at it and you love it. I'd never ask you to give that up. It's too much part of who you are. It's too much part of what makes us love you."

"But. . ."

"I didn't mean that *you* had to be the one to bring change, Kathy. Get over yourself." Bobby nudged her jokingly. "I'm gonna reduce my workload. *I'm* gonna spend more time at home. *I'll* do the majority of the childcare and household stuff."

Kathy's eyes filled with emotion.

Bobby's face was matter of fact.

"I'm better at all that stuff than you are anyway, love." he shrugged. "You do what you're good at and I will too. Sound fair?"

Tears final breaking free to run down her cheeks, Kathy McGuire nodded emphatically.

"Good," Bobby asserted. "Just try to keep yourself out of harm's way in future."

Kathy reached out her arms, like a child, inviting him to embrace.

Closing her arms around him, she ignored the pain in her side and pulled him close.

"God, I love you, Bobby McGuire."

"Love you too, m'darlin'."

Interlude…

The Guardian:

> **Tequila Mockingbird's campaign is not only justified, but a natural and proportionate response to the seemingly unchangeable tide of oppression perpetuated for far too long by a patriarchal society.**

Newly emerged, if not newly active, serial killer Tequila Mockingbird has exploded into global consciousness in recent days. Whilst many, perhaps rightly, denounce her methods – after all, who could condone the taking of human life – many more have raised their online voices in support of a woman who has taken it upon herself to punish abusive and violent men. Women in particular, but not exclusively, have rushed to comment on, debate and yes, support the killing of men who even Police Scotland confirm have abused their partners for years.

Miranda Scoone, firebrand-editor of online women's rights magazine, *Women Matter*, has been forthright and loud in her admiration of Tequila. In an editorial, Scoone asserted:

'Tequila Mockingbird is weeding the chauvinist garden. In taking the power from these men and punishing them in the very manner they have chosen to treat the women in their lives, Tequila is sending a clear message to men who think that women and their bodies are properties to be managed and used. Tequila's mission, when viewed in a historical context, is a natural, proportionate and entirely justified progression of the mission and values of Emmeline Pankhurst and her comrades.'

In response to the question, 'Surely a less violent method of exposing and shaming these men would have been preferable?' Miranda replied:

'Absolutely not. Violence is the only language men like this know and respond to. Men like these have been victimising and controlling women for centuries in this manner. That a woman is equipped to stand up and, metaphorically speaking, talk to them in their own tongue is not only admirable, but utterly desirable at this point in history.'

'Rape, discrimination, female genital mutilation, gender pay gaps, and domestic abuse. These are not things of the past, they happen every minute of every day, in every country of the world. Nothing has changed this in the history of human beings. Not the Suffragettes, not two World Wars, during which women effectively ran the logistics of the UK in the absence of their men and certainly not the endless stream of politicians who merely pay lip-service to equality of any type. What Tequila is doing is shouting loudly above the din of apathy and acceptance. She is demanding that we see what she is trying to show us. That the thin gossamer of progress is a lie. That perhaps a culling of the sex who have always been so cruelly and relentlessly destructive is past due.'

***

BBC News:

Crazed lady serial killer stalks Britain's men.

Doctor of Psychology, Professor Campbell asserts:

'This *Tequila Mockingbird* woman has embarked upon a wholly immoral mission to punish men whom she alone judges to be guilty of what are, let's be honest, minor crimes when compared to her own. Even if these men were guilty of domestic abuse, which none of them incidentally have even been charged with, much less been found guilty of in a court of law, that would not merit their lives being taken from them.'

The Young Turks:

Heroic feminist-icon, or insane serial killer?

The New York Times:

Has 21st century society created Tequila Mockingbird?

The Huffington Post:

Mockingbird sings a song of brutality, but is it one we need to hear?

The Onion:

Man who's never cooked for his wife writes an open letter apologising to Tequila Mockingbird.

Liberty Is Life:

Kill 'em all? That's her answer? Meet violence with violence? Mete out murder to deter? Whoever this 'Tequila Mockingbird' may claim to be, she's no better than the men she destroys. Snuffing out one life to save others? That's the male method of getting things done. It's a Neolithic approach to gender politics – just find a bigger stick and smite your opponent with it.

True liberation lies in education, of both sexes. Fear, retribution and revenge, those are the tools of the male oppressor, wielded to such monstrous effect over millennia that even intelligent women think they must take up cudgels to achieve anything. Lay down your sword, sister. When the only tool you possess is a hammer, everything looks like a nail. Stop hammering and find your humanity.

Superbitch:

Why bother? Why bother 'saving' these whining miserable breeders? What's Tequila going to do next – kiss them better and read them a bedtime story? Look after them for the rest of their lives? These women could walk away at any time.

They could stand up for themselves. But they don't. They don't have the spine. Doesn't she realise they'll just crawl into bed alongside the next strong man who offers them protection and attention?

She Devil:

The only thing Tequila's doing wrong is she's not killing enough of these fuckers. They think they own us – they don't for one minute believe women are equal to men. They smile like the two-faced shits they really are and making nice noises about maternity leave and workplace equality and blah blah blah . . . when really, they're just looking at our tits and dreaming of the next blow job. Deep down, they're all abusers. Even the ones who don't actually hit you – they're all thinking the same thing. They're rapists in waiting, every one of them. She should cut their cocks off and leave them to bleed out.

Now...

21

It's really happening

For perhaps the sixth time in the last half hour I've spent scanning news and sifting through social media feeds, commenting as Tequila and responding to messages of support, the thought has surfaced bringing a smile to my lips. The BBC have been running a constant reel on the murders, dating right back to the first blog I posted. A series of talking heads, shrinks, medical examiners, cops and serial-killer experts have rotated throughout the day, airing their opinions, some of which I can't help but agree with, while others make me prickle with their naivety and willingness to trivialise. In five minutes viewing, the BBC's guests have referred to me as a *monster, the worst kind of woman, a crusader, deranged* and *a predator.*

Sky are running with the *maniac* angle and have focused on the *innocent* men I've apparently robbed of their dignity and lives. Online views, comments, threads, blogs, articles, opinion pieces and tweets are simply infinite in the sheer number of them and the range in opinions.

Many voice their encouragement and support. A few have formed a group named *I am Tequila.* They offer to take my place, take responsibility for my *crimes,* even go to prison in my place, for the cause.

Many more hurl abuse and threats via their one-hundred and forty characters. Some profess to patrol the streets, hunting me. Others threaten to kill or torture or rape me. I've had seventeen hundred marriage proposals.

MPs denounce my actions, but stress the need for a frank and in depth conversation on equality.

The debate is really happening. I've made them talk about it. Whether I can make them care enough to act, I have no way of assessing.

With a view of the lockers beneath Camden Lock, I skim my eyes between the news and media feeds scrolling across the screen of my white phone and the locker I've directed Stevenson's spouse to. I delivered my note and watched while he absorbed the words and reacted earlier today. That means I'm here for the next few hours at least. I've a meeting with my publisher in a couple of hours. If the spouse hasn't turned up by then, I'll reluctantly make my way to the publisher's offices in the West End, then work my way back to the locker in Camden as soon as I can manage. Not ideal, but I don't have any real choice. If I miss the pickup, I'll just have to head to the airport and try to locate the spouse.

If the locker is empty, I'll give it twelve hours and make sure he's not returning home before I hunt Stevenson. I have all I need prepped in the AirBnB flat I rented under an alias. I can be ready for the early hours and the kill to come, if the opportunity comes along. If the locker is still untouched, I'll wait some more, I guess.

Not for the first time since I boarded my flight to London the day before, I sit second-guessing the choices I've made. Better judgement, as well as habit, dictates that I shouldn't be acting as I am, moving a kill up so soon after McCabe, much less two kills. The media engagement though, is simply too strong to ignore. This is the moment I've planned for: it'll never come again. These next two kills will push them to where I need them to be. Scared, angry, desperate to stop me. I'm way off-script, a maverick in my own carefully constructed life, moving through the minutes and hours free of the meticulous methods that have kept me safe and dangerous, for so long.

Having had Stevenson's kill planned for six months now, as well as Gavin Watson's, who is next on the list, I have everything I need to instil confidence in executing the kills to come.

I know without doubt that these men are guilty of abusing their partners. I know their routines, the manner in which they move. I know their homes, their habits and their lives. I'm prepared, as always; flawless. But this time I'm going straight from one kill to another and then another, far too soon for comfort.

I shrug off the doubt. The two kills to come are hundreds of miles apart. I'm prepped and I'm ready for them and two more besides if I need to. I can do this. I must.

"This Tequila thing though?" A woman's voice, southern-North American accent, takes hold of my attention.

Two women in their forties stroll towards me. On their lunchbreak, they each have a coffee in hand. Taking the bench to my right, the redhead, in an ankle-length skirt and plain black T, performs a series of intricate gestures that smack of the upper-classes, inviting her friend to skooch closer against the cold. Despite her obvious warmth towards her companion, the redhead has an evident, light-hearted cynicism.

Her friend, shoulder-length brown hair with just a couple of silvers showing, wears jeans and a Tbearing a quote I don't recognise, over an athletic build. The brunette is one of those types who, despite being seated comfortably, is in constant motion, like she's left her engine idling. Her foot taps absent-mindedly against the bench leg. She speaks with her hands.

Together they have that easy manner, sometimes conspiratorial, occasionally acerbic, that only old friends develop. I like them both instantly.

Huddled close, they sip at their drinks, discussing Tequila Mockingbird.

"I'd like to say that I'm appalled, right? I mean, we're talking about a fucking serial killer here. And, you know, murder is wrong." The brunette rolls her eyes to punctuate.

A wry smile tugs at the corners of Redhead's lips. "If you say so."

Her friend notes the pre-grin, but proceeds unabashed.

"But I can't help but think that if Mockingbird had been around when I was a kid, Miss Brenda might still be around instead of dead from a fucking aneurysm because that piece of shit beat her so hard that a blood vessel broke in her fucking head. And her kids might not have grown up all fucked up. You know, that asshole didn't even serve five fucking years."

An elderly man passing by gapes at the brunette's language. My instant affection for her increases exponentially. The women are oblivious to the man's disapproval.

"Five years?" Redhead asks, sceptically.

Brunette throws her hands up. "Fucking manslaughter. It was the seventies. Wife-beating was illegal, but no one really took it seriously then. He went to jail for beating her *too hard*. . . not for beating her."

"God, I loathe people," Redhead enunciates.

Nodding her acqui esce, Brunette continues.

"What's really fucked up is that ultimately this Mockingbird chick probably isn't doing any good. Women in abusive relationships are pretty broken, y' know. If you're not, you just don't stay in that position. So they'll probably just move on to some other abuser."

Redhead eyes her friend. Humour clashes with scepticism once again.

"Only now they're even more fucked up with survivor's guilt on top of everything else. So the next guy might even be worse." Brunette's foot taps a little more slowly.

Redhead leans over to remove some lint from her friend's jacket. "I wouldn't say she isn't doing *any* good. Those men are dead. That's certainly an improvement."

Brunette shrugs. "Fair enough. . . Some of them had kids, right? She might have saved the kids in the end. Or fucked them up worse. . . It's hard to say."

A mental tug takes my attention from them, tuning me out from their exchange. Chance makes me look up at the locker, mostly because I've cocked my head in its direction to scratch under my wig. I almost miss him. He looks so different from the last time I checked in on the couple. David Grayson, spouse of Bill

Stevenson. Where a young, athletically-slim man with carefully unkempt dark hair, bright blue eyes and casual gentleness once stood, the David before me is a pale, sunken-eyed, scruffy shade of himself.

God, the kid looks terrible. He's lost at least ten pounds from a frame that could have ill-afforded to lose two pounds. I watch him rummage through the locker, his darkly circled eyes widening with each object he finds. He has his head partly in the locker so his body blocks my view of what he's doing, but the very instant he reads his letter, I know. He steps back from the locker, both hands covering his mouth. His face and eyes are puffy and sodden with tears. I watch him take all of fifteen seconds to make his decision.

Straightening his back, this twenty-something kid, all but destroyed, cowed and shredded to a quaking child by the man he loves, lifts his head, searches around with tired, grateful eyes then vanishes from my sight, the rucksack I left for him over one shoulder, my letter clutched in a fist.

A wide, malevolent grin forms on my face. I can't help it, nor do I really care enough to wipe it from my face. This one, Bill Stevenson, he's one of the lowest bastards I've encountered for years. The things he's done to this kid, the dignity he's taken from him, have earned Stevenson a special regard from me.

My step significantly lighter than it has been, I set off for the Tube station and a meeting that no longer seems the inconvenience it once did.

***

Tequila Mockingbird
Blog
Kill 19

Bill Stevenson is dead. He has only himself to blame. Bill married a young man half his age. He married him because he wanted someone to control. Someone who loved him and someone from whom he could demand unconditional loyalty and dedication. David Grayson is a gentle soul. A very young man who was groomed by Bill Stevenson in a manner consistent with his type of abuser. Bill showered David with gifts and affection. He swept the kid off his feet. They married very quickly and the violence began soon after.

The charming older man who seemed to worship David vanished, replaced by a demanding bully who controlled almost every aspect of David's life. Friends, family, even a career, these things slowly vanished from David's life as Bill intimidated, dominated and manipulated David into submitting to him. David's world was shrunk down to whatever Bill deemed appropriate. If David strayed from the rules, Bill would punish his husband.

He was a very careful abuser. The bruises never showed to anyone who still cared enough after Bill had removed most of David's family and friends from their lives.

David lived three full years in constant fear of failing Bill and of suffering his punishment for doing so. The fourth year of his marriage, David stopped dreading the beatings and the rapes. He knew, he'd learned by that stage, that he deserved the violence.

David is free now and completely blameless in his husband's death.

I killed Bill in his home. With a mouthful of his own amputated fingers, he screamed his way to the hereafter as I plunged a very large, cold blade slowly through his rear ribs into his heart. He died a coward, as all bullies do, screaming his sorries amidst the occasional promise to kill me.

David played no role in Bill's death. I acted alone.

I know these things about Bill Stevenson, I punished Bill Stevenson because I watched him for a long time. I saw how he destroyed those he should have loved and cherished.

Bill will never harm David or anyone else again.

Press In,

Tequila

I publish the blog and watch the read count hit more than one million within one minute of it going live. Abruptly an alien thought occurs. The police, news agencies, men and women who've signed up to my Twitter feed, Facebook page or blog, in almost every country and city in the world, will know I've killed again. The police have his name. They'll be on their way to the kill site in moments.

A thrill races through me at the realisation that my kill will be discovered immediately. That the forensics team will be on scene within hours instead of days as has been the case until now.

Once again, the notion occurs. *This is really happening. This is it.*

Removing all news and media feeds from my screen, I open a Word document and begin the process of scrutinising a letter I've edited endlessly for eight years now. In those years, the document, let's call it a mission statement, has gone from a thirty-thousand-word manuscript to a much more succinct statement of intent:

I will execute one more abuser. Following his death, you have five years to the very day. In that time, I will not kill again. I will ignore every instinct I possess, every shove, fist, threat and foot from an abuser. You in turn will ensure that new legislation to protect abused spouses and appropriately punish those perpetrating the abuse is introduced to more effectively address the needs of the victim and the callousness of the abuser.

I demand that a special summit is held with representatives from all the G7 countries present. I further demand that your summit reach an accord and a plan of action for the active and vigorous promotion and improvements of women's rights and equality.

I want laws in place or in the process of being put in place that protect the families. That prevent women from being discriminated against or abused in any way. Abusers have been empowered and protected for far too long. It's time to take that power from them. It's time to force true equality upon a society that so clearly does not value or want it.

If five years pass and no measurable progress has been made, I will make my presence felt on a much larger scale.

Press In,
Tequila

Satisfied with its contents, I cut and paste it into the body of an email I've prepped with around three hundred recipients. Police forces throughout Europe and the United States, news agencies, women's rights groups, high profile blogs, MPs, MSPs, EU Ministers, senators and congressmen and women: all of them will receive my email with a click. A thought tugs at me and I add one more address into the top box, smiling to myself as I click send. DI Kathy McGuire.

A growing sense of something concluding has become more noticeable to me the last few days. It's quite something, seeing your life's work reach fruition. With an appreciative sigh, I stretch my arms above my head, popping a few creaky vertebrae. A tug at the cut on my upper arm reminds me sharply not to stretch too far.

I roll my sleeve up to inspect the small wound on my upper arm. For the life of me I can't figure out when or where I cut myself. The tears in my outer suit and plastic under-suit, tell me I did it in Stevenson's home. How or when I cannot know and must assume that forensics will find some of my blood at the scene. The insight brings a similar rush to what I experienced when I discovered that my blog had become mainstream. Nothing I can do about it now; nothing except trust in my plan and preparation.

22

Kathy's eyes scan around the conference room assessing the mood and the intentions of those gathered. Steve, one foot on a bin, his rear end resting on a desk, is relaxed as ever and chatting idly to the Chief Super, McBride, about the weekend's rugby results. The Super himself looks tired, but otherwise seems in fine fettle. He's fairly open-minded for a man in his position, but the political pressure he is surely experiencing is most likely the reason for his creased forehead and sunken eyes. He okayed Kathy's request to keep Tequila's blog and twitter feed online, but he's undoubtedly now having second thoughts.

DCI Charley Donnelly is a virtual storm of malicious intent, held in check only by the presence of the Chief Super. Kathy can feel his eyes fixed on her, but so far has refused to make eye contact. Donnelly is itching to get the meeting started and most likely give Steve and Kathy the hairdryer treatment. After a few more minutes of listening to his teeth grind, the Super takes a break in Steve's chatter to call us together.

Despite the coming battle, Kathy lets out a relieved sigh.

"Well, folks," he booms, clapping his hands together. "Shall we get this started?"

Kathy exchanges a quick meaningful glance with Steve. Wordlessly they acknowledge Donnelly's mood, offering each other a reassuring nod.

Donnelly takes the centre of the room as the Super seats himself with a weary groan.

"To summarise," the Super begins without preamble or niceties, "we have a serial who would appear to have killed, what, fifteen innocent men?"

"Nineteen now, sir," Steve interjects. "If her blog is accurate."

Donnelly's eyebrows rise in a mocking gesture. "Oh, why wouldn't it be, Sergeant? A killer, who claims to be female, posts details about each of the kills, linking them together, claiming them as her work and we accept that as evidence in this force now, do we?"

Steve flicks his eyes to the Super who is sitting forward attentively. A tight, flat grin threatens on Steve's lips.

"As you will have read in our reports, Constable Gilmour has independently inked the crimes, days before the blog emerged in fact, by cross-referencing the UK force's crime databases." Steve lets his words hang for a few moments, allowing the time for a slight twitch to tic on Donnelly's cheek.

Kathy notes that the Super looks unimpressed.

Donnelly decides to brazen it out. "Of course, Sergeant, but my point still stands: a few coincidences of MO and target do not make a solid case."

"The blogs contain details of the murders that none of the forces investigating released to the public, sir," Kathy adds. "We're convinced that the author of the blog is the killer. Gilmour's research backs that up."

Donnelly steps towards her, but is halted mid-stride by the Super's deep voice.

"For God's sake, Charley. Save the pissing contest for another day. If reprimands are justified, rest assured they'll be forthcoming once we have the killer in custody."

The Super's eyes lose their characteristic warmth and bore into Donnelly's for a brief moment, before moving to meet Kathy's.

"Kathy, I believe that Charley is rather miffed and considerably doubtful about your decision to allow this Tequila any more media time, so to speak. As am I." The Super sits back in to his chair, but his eyes remain sternly fixed on Kathy. "My patience for this strategy is thinning, on that matter Charley and I are in agreement."

Gesturing to the floor with an open hand, the Super invites Kathy to report.

Wishing Gilmour was here, Kathy steps to the little smart board and retrieves the remote.

"Thank you, sirs," she says clicking the PowerPoint into action. "As DC Gilmour relayed in his reports," Kathy glances at Donnelly for a split second, long enough to catch his eyes dart guiltily to the side, "we have a consistent MO across all fifteen of the cases he managed to link. Of the remaining murders detailed in Tequila's blog, we discovered the same types of wounds, same professional manner and in nine cases now, distilled water on or around the victim."

Taking a pause to allow processing time, Kathy notes that Steve has resumed his relaxed posture.

"We have also found what appear to be similarly ice-burned wounds in nine of the cases."

"What appear to be?" Donnelly interrupts.

"Yes. As some of the cases are several years old, all we have to go on are the photos taken by the medical examiner in each case. Dr Ferguson has examined the wounds of every case and consulted with each of the professionals involved in the post-mortems. He's comfortably certain that nine of the men were killed with the same weapon as McKenna, McCabe and Stevenson."

"Ah, Ferguson's *ice weapon*," the Super says, doubt lacing his tone.

Kathy acknowledges his scepticism with a smile. "I had the same reaction when he proposed the idea to me, sir, but look here." Kathy flips through a series of images and short videos. "Dr Ferguson blew up these images for us, as well as those from our three recent victims. Note the ragged and discoloured edges of the wounds, here, here and here." Kathy points out the various wounds, noting that the Super is leaning forward again to scrutinise them. Even Donnelly is scanning the images intently.

"No doubt the wounds were caused by the same weapon, most likely utilised by the same person, but ice?" Donnelly snorts his derision in punctuation.

Ignoring her superior, Kathy focuses on the Super whilst bringing more images onto the screen.

"This is a similar wound that Dr Ferguson made himself, with a kitchen knife."

An image of a slab of pig flank with a wound piercing the skin and flesh shows on the screen. Kathy replaces it with a second picture of a wound, once again on pigskin. The Super is on his feet, closing the distance between himself and the screen to better assess the photo.

"This looks like the wounds on the murder victims," he says with certainty.

Kathy nods. "Dr Ferguson made that wound using an ice blade he fashioned to roughly match the size he calculates the murder weapon to be."

The temptation to steal a glance at Donnelly's face is almost overwhelming. A hissing laugh from Steve tells her that Donnelly is apoplectic.

Stepping forward to come shoulder to shoulder with the Super, Kathy traces the wound's edges with a finger.

"This is more ragged, sir and the ice burn is more severe, but there's no mistaking that ice is likely the material the murder weapon is made from."

"There are differences that cannot be discounted though, Kathy," Donnelly says.

"Yes, sir. Dr Ferguson moulded his blade in a piece of plastic and he didn't use distilled water. We have no idea of the temperature our killer would set the ice blades at, we don't know the type of moulds she uses, or how she fashions a handle that is usable. With these variables in mind and the likelihood that Tequila is simply more skilled at making these blades than Dr Ferguson, we are confident that the differences between Ferguson's wounds and the ones made by the killer can be reliably put down to his relative lack of skill in making ice weapons."

Suddenly aware that the room is entirely silent, Kathy locks eyes with each of her colleagues in turn. Steve bobs his head in approval. Donnelly's anger has abated and seems to have been replaced by reluctant approval. The Chief Super looks impressed.

"This is great work, Kathy," he offers. "You too, Steve."

Both nod their thanks.

"Gilmour really got us on the correct track, sir," Kathy says, soliciting an appreciative nod from the Super.

Recovering himself, the Super juts his chin over at Donnelly. "What are your thoughts, Charley?" he asks, inviting the DCI to take the floor.

Nodding thoughtfully, Donnelly stays where he is, but lifts his hands in a more open gesture than he's displayed so far.

"This is quite a stack of evidence, overwhelming really. Your team has done magnificent work joining the dots on such a unique case. Some great police work has been put in on this."

A sidelong glance at Steve's expression tells Kathy he's also waiting on the '*but*'.

"However," Donnelly continues, "despite the impressive input from your team and Dr Ferguson, we have in fact no clues as to the identity of this Tequila. We have no solid leads to assist us in finding her, and we have allowed this person to brag of her heinous acts of violence to anyone with an internet connection."

His face sympathetic, the Super adds, "It was a bad decision, Kathy, and one Charley and I played a part in, but this Tequila's blog needs shut down now. Keeping it live simply hasn't offered any leads and is most likely of detriment to our case at this stage. It is certainly of detriment to our reputation as a police force."

Kathy lets out a long breath she hadn't been aware she'd been holding.

"I understand, sir and on a normal case, I would agree, but this is a unique situation. Our killer is simply too professional, too prepared and too dedicated at this point to fall victim to the mistakes that aid us in tracking normal serials. She is meticulous. Aside from the distilled water, which is practically useless as physical evidence and the odd synthetic hair from wigs available in any number of places across Europe she does not leave a trace of her presence."

"And the dead men, of course," Donnelly interrupts gruffly.

Kathy concedes his point with a tight nod.

"She doesn't kill in anger, the wounds she inflicts are precise, almost surgical. She selects her targets and apparently has them under surveillance for months. She makes damn sure that she is killing people who fit a very specific profile."

"Each and every victim she has *selected* has been someone who has never been convicted of a crime," the Super adds.

"That's true," Kathy agrees, "but even a cursory cross-reference from Gilmour demonstrated a likely pattern of injuries and minor incidents which suggests domestic violence in each case."

Kathy raises her hands in a placatory gesture in response to Donnelly's move to speak.

"I'm not suggesting she has a right, I'm merely pointing out her MO and that she obviously has a consistent code of ethics she maintains that make sense to her."

"What's your point, Kathy?" Donnelly asks, clearly tiring of her monologue.

"My point, sir, is that we're not going to catch her without this line of communication left open for her. She wants to tell us her story. She wants to make a statement. So let's communicate with her. Let's get her talking."

The room falls silent again for a few long moments. Finally Steve speaks. "We've never had an opportunity like this with a serial before. An open line of dialogue. An explanation of her motives. We had officers on scene at the Stevenson kill within thirty minutes of her blog publishing. We've never had a glut of fresh evidence like that before. Sirs, with respect, I think we'd be fucking mental to break that link."

Kathy nods her support. Flicking her eyes between Donnelly and the Super, she cannot assess their frame of mind from their expressions.

Taking a seat, Kathy allows some of the tension to leave her muscles. They've done what they can, her superiors will decide how they proceed now.

"Would you mind giving Charley and I a moment to confer?" Phrasing it as a question rather than an order, out of courtesy, the Super nods to the door.

As they leave, Gilmour races towards the conference room, file in hand.

Steve steps towards him, accepting the offered file. As Steve reads the contents, young Gilmour grins broadly at Kathy. A few moments later, Steve's face breaks into the same goofy grin.

"Forensics found blood at the Stevenson home. Unidentified, it doesn't belong to Stevenson or his husband, Grayson. Ferguson reckons it must belong to our killer. Seems she caught an arm on a wardrobe door. Just a nick, Ferguson says, but enough to get some DNA from. No match yet from the database."

Before Kathy can reply, Donnelly storms through the doors behind them and along the hallway, straight out of the main exit.

"Guess we get to keep the blog live a while longer," Kathy says playfully.

"C'mon. Let's go tell the Super about our new lead."

Then...

23

Seated in the first-class lounge, I'd been reading some celeb magazine whiling the time away, awaiting my flight. Drawn by a flicker of the departures board, I noted that my Aer Lingus flight was now boarding. I left the lounge, emerging into the thoroughfare of the main terminal.

Edinburgh Airport buzzed with stressed executives, flustered parents, excited school kids and weary long-haulers. On the periphery of all of them I hugged my cramping belly and sipped at my coffee, observing the maelstrom. A calm detachment affected me. I felt in control and decisive. Dressed crisply in newly bought attire and sporting a freshly dyed new, neat haircut, I was possessed of a confidence and sense of purpose. Fear or regret simply did not exist for me in that moment. Despite the growing cramps in my gut, I felt truly aware of and free from the world around me.

A seasoned traveller, I had negotiated security and passport control with little fuss. *Headed back home, Ms Kinney? This way to the gate, Ms Kinney.*

My passport held a photo that was almost ten years old. I'd been meaning to update it, but it hadn't seemed urgent. Now, aside from a paling of my face, the image was an almost perfect representation of my newly-groomed and attired self.

Content, I'd strolled to my gate, a single rucksack as my baggage, over my shoulder lightly. Mercifully, my first-class ticket ensured that my wait to board was short. My cramps had escalated significantly. So much so that by the time I'd been seated, I wished for nothing more than to curl up in my seat, with the aid of some codeine and sleep.

My recurring cramps woke me many hours later. My underwear felt wet despite the maternity pad. Pressure in my ears told me that we were descending. I wished for nothing more than to ignore the need to change my underwear. For the ghastly reminder of Nicole to be gone from my person. Someone had kindly placed a soft fleece blanket over me as I'd slept. Wrapping it around my shoulders, I fetched my bag and headed for the bathroom to clean up before landing.

A young steward enquired after my health. I recall gruffly brushing him off needlessly, simply because I felt I may pass out if I didn't reach another seat immediately. The bathroom remained my sanctuary whilst I cleaned up and waited for the world to stop spinning. The steward eventually had to demand that I return to my seat, which I did reluctantly, apologising for my shortness with him.

Following our arrival, I went directly to the airport bathrooms to change my entire outfit. I ditched my clothes, redressing in a new set. I undid my hair, allowing it to flow free, then covered my crown with a soft hat. My rucksack I disposed of, keeping only its meagre contents which I stuffed into the pockets of my coat.

On exiting the airport and with the aid of an information clerk, I boarded a tram, Seb's address clutched tightly in my fist. At odds with the mild temperature, sweat was a frost on my back. Fevered, I shook in my seat, shifting closer to the window to absorb the heat of the sun.

"Ma'am, this is your stop," the driver called over his shoulder to me in reply to my earlier request.

I thanked him and alighted onto Frederick Street, Cole Valley. The steep gradient of the street disoriented me for several minutes. Stood, hand braced against a telegraph pole for stability, I moved my eyes along the row of houses lining the leafy street, searching for Seb's house.

Realising that his house was merely three buildings from me, I fixed my eyes intently on his front door, partly for motivation, mostly to aid in ignoring the loose swaying world around me. Several times as I made my way to Seb's door, sweat blurred my vision. Hours seemed to pass. My fevered head pounded. I vomited. . . twice. My eyes refused to focus.

At length, I reached his porch. My trembling, frosty-jointed limbs gave out, sending me sprawling heavily and unguarded onto my face.

It was early evening, on a Saturday. Knowing Seb, as I do now, I realise how lucky I was and how uncharacteristic it was, for him to be home. He'd opened his door and then the screen, rushing to my side. Coming down on one knee, he surveyed my shaking, broken self.

Through a haze of pain-filled fever and claggy thoughts, I recall him asking who I was. I'd laughed at that, on the inside at least.

"It's me, Seb," I'd asserted, puzzled. "It's Alice."

Moving my matted hair back from my face, Seb pressed at my forehead with the back of his hand. I felt his eyes move over me, assessing my condition. I was fevered, beaten and suffering from a uterine infection that might have killed me. Still, I was pissed at him for not recognising me.

His eyes met mine. I watched him wearily. Looking at my face and into my eyes, he visibly started, recognising me. So I thought, at any rate.

"You look like Alice," he said, softly. "But you aren't." There was no malice or even judgement in his voice, his tone was respectful but brooked no debate.

With the last of my fading strength and consciousness, I roared at him, "What's wrong with you, Seb? It's me. Alice Kinney."

I thrust the crumpled page of my diary at him. He read his own address in my handwriting. Something inscrutable to me, some decision he made, passed over his features. "Okay. . . Alice. Let's get you some help."

With sweaty grasping hands, I pulled his face towards my own. "No police," I moaned. "New identity. Move my money. Pay in cash. Been trouble. . . at home. My sister. . ." I grabbed at his arm roughly. "I'm Alice. . . just Alice. You know me."

Seb picked me up into his arms as easily as if I were a child. "That's fine, *Alice*," he placated me. "Whatever you wish."

The world retreated into merciful unconsciousness.

24

The doorbell chime woke Kathy from a slumber she hadn't intended to take. To either side of her on the couch, her kids lay drowsing. Kathy couldn't recall the last time she'd spent as much quality time with them as she had this last fortnight or so since she'd been allowed home to recuperate. It couldn't last. Work would return to break their bubble once again, but for that moment Kathy was determined to simply be with her family.

"How's it going, pal?" Jackson's voice drifted in from the hallway, along with a chill evening breeze. The kids snuggled closer to her warmth.

"Yeah, not bad," Bobby replied. "You here to see Kathy?"

"Aye."

"Come away in, then. I'll get the kids out of your way, let you two talk."

Kathy's brow furrowed. What she'd assumed was a chance visit had plainly been planned, judging by the men's exchange.

Both men entered the living room, exchanging guilty glances at each other.

"You two look like you're going to the headmaster's office," Kathy said.

Jackson's eyes darted to the left. He placed a briefcase he'd been carrying near the skirting at the door.

"Eh, aye. . . sorry Mc. . . Kathy. I asked Bobby if I could come around and y'know. . . clear the air."

Puzzled, Kathy cocked her head to the side. "Clear the air? No need, Steve. We're good."

Jackson nodded, but his expression betrayed his true feelings.

"Yeah, but there's something we need. . . I need to talk with you about, Kathy. If that's okay."

Kathy shrugged. Glancing to her husband, she noted that he was eager for her and Jackson to talk.

Encouraging her, he gathered the kids up. Half-asleep, they flopped, one over each shoulder, legs and arms wrapped around their dad as he carted them out of the living room and upstairs.

Jackson shifted his feet uncomfortably eliciting a laugh from Kathy.

"For God's sake, Steve. You look like you're waiting for a court appearance." Gesturing at the seat nearby her, Kathy invited him to sit.

"You need anything?" he asked, hovering above the seat.

"No, thanks Steve. Just sit down, will you? You're making me twitchy."

Fussing with a cushion behind him, Steve eventually sat. Back straight, face concerned, he looked as far from comfortable as Kathy had seen him.

"Kathy, I wanted to say how grateful I am that you put yourself in harm's way for me."

Kathy held a hand up as though to silence Jackson.

"We've been over this, Steve. No need. You'd have done the same for me."

His eyes were wide now. "Yes, I would have," he said earnestly. "I should've been quicker to react through, I. . ." Jackson's eyes lowered. "I allowed myself to lose my temper."

"It's not your fault, Steve," Kathy said.

"I could've killed that boy, Kathy." His eyes could not meet hers for a moment.

"But you didn't," Kathy comforted him.

Finally, his eyes met hers. Rimmed in red, sunken in black shadows, they looked like he hadn't slept for weeks. "I could've got you killed too, Kathy."

"But you didn't," she said, her tone mirroring her earlier statement. "I'm here, and I'm fine, Steve."

Steve nodded once. He looked like a man who couldn't accept what he saw in front of him, like a person whose memories of an event had skewed and darkened everything in their life.

Kathy reached out for him. Placing a hand on his knee, she flooded her voice with genuine sympathy, affection and forgiveness.

"It wasn't ideal, Steve, but we got through it. No-one expects you to be perfect. We did what we had to do. Neither of us could've prevented Graham's death and we were there for each other. That's all I can ask of my partner."

Jackson's eyes locked on hers. The red around them had deepened. Tears welled.

"I haven't been there for you Kathy. I haven't treated you as an equal, let alone my partner." Jackson's chin tremored slightly. "I've been boorish, a bully. I've been isolated and resentful and I've treated you with disdain. I've been a fool. Can you forgive me?"

"No question," Kathy said without hesitation. "And thank you, Steve. That must've been difficult for you."

"No," he replied emphatically. Tears fell freely now. "It wasn't difficult at all."

Moments passed. They composed themselves, making small talk and catching up on office goings-on and gossip.

Kathy remembered the briefcase he had with him.

"What do you have in there?" she asked, nodding over at the case.

Steve raised an eyebrow. Humour danced in his eyes.

"Oh, that? That's for you, Kathy."

Retrieving his case, he unlatched the buckle and emptied a file onto his lap. Kathy's brow furrowed as she watched him open it.

"Here you go," he said, holding the open file out for her. "I reckoned you'd be getting bored at home by now." Steve smiled as Kathy scanned the first page of the document he'd brought.

"Sergeant's exam?"

Steve nodded. "Yeah. It's about time, don't you think?"

Kathy's smile flattened. "Steve, I appreciate the thought, but I. . . I just don't think so. Not just now."

"Why not?" he asked.

"Steve, I—"

Jackson leaned in to cut her off. "Kathy you're an excellent detective and a natural leader. This is right for you, trust me."

Kathy acknowledged his support with a tight nod, then shook her head.

"Steve, being a woman in the force is difficult. I have to work twice as hard to get half the recognition and that's fine. . . but right now, after all this? I just don't have the energy."

Jackson stood. Coming down on one knee in front of her, he looked at her with regret and great sincerity.

"I'm sorry that I've been part of that, but those days are over. You have to work twice as hard to get half the credit? So fucking what? Work four times as hard then and be the standout of our department you naturally are."

His eyes searched hers. Noting a flicker of interest, he seized upon it.

"I'll be there, every step of the way. Full partners, Kathy. We get each other's backs."

Kathy's stoic demeanour began to melt away.

"It's time to move on, Kathy. It's time to show them all what you're worth."

Kathy's eyes widened, then narrowed as she considered her response.

"Yeah, I suppose it is, Sergeant Jackson."

Now...

25

"Alice, I really believe that one more book in the series could take your books up another level, perhaps make the collection a genuine rival for *Harry Potter*. You're almost there now."

David is leaning forward, giving me the big puppy dog eyes. His performance is somewhat adorable, but mostly it's exhausting.

David has come all the way up to Glasgow to meet with me, at his own insistence, despite my having spent two hours in conference with his team in London recently. He's not a bad bloke, for a publisher. Really he's just doing his job, trying to get as large a market for the *Vampire Junior High* books as possible. What he can't accept is that I'm done with them.

It doesn't help, of course, that my focus is elsewhere at present. The media interest in my Tequila blog and my kills has grown exponentially. News channels run every detail of each kill on a continuous feed. Reconstructions and CGI expositions of my kills dominate. Surprisingly, some of them are fairly accurate. Experts psychoanalyse me and my methods. I listened to a crime historian on Radio Two draw comparisons between my willingness to communicate and the notes sent to the Whitechapel police during Jack the Ripper's reign. Satisfyingly, many, many voices are being raised in support of my actions.

The white phone buzzes in my bag. I have it set so that only certain notifications come through, otherwise its battery would be dead in an hour. My guess is that I've had another message from DI McGuire. She's persistent, I'll give her that and punctual.

Every hour she sends me the same message.

Tequila, we want to understand and help you. Please talk to us.

Despite the media attention my cause is receiving, the need to speak openly and honestly, perhaps even to vent one on one, even over instant message, is tempting. It's a distraction and a risk I can ill afford. Inevitably I'd give too much of myself away.

My attention drawn reluctantly back to the room, I focus my eyes more certainly on David's face.

"David, we've been over this," I say flatly. "There won't be any more books in the series; most likely I won't write in that genre again."

"That's just crazy, Alice," he pleads. "Do you have any idea how many writers would do anything to be in the position you are?"

I narrow my eyes and allow a chill to pass between us.

"I do. Better than you do, David. The success I've had with these books is the writer's equivalent of winning the goddamn lottery. It only happens for an incredibly small percentage. Most writers can't even earn a modest living from doing the thing they love most. Most of them write better books than mine to boot."

"Exactly, Alice," David pushes. "This is a once-every-twenty-years phenomenon. Walking away from it is. . . well, why would you?"

Part of me wants to squash him, show him exactly how little I care about him making a few million less on the millions my books have already brought in for his company. Mostly I just want him to drop it.

"David, I understand that this series is the golden goose you publishers scavenge for and fight over to discover, but you and I both know that selling books in these numbers is about luck, being marketable in the right genre at the right time and maybe, lastly, having a decent book."

I throw him a look that stops him from interrupting.

"This last book is exactly that."

He sinks into his chair a little more heavily. "Will you at least consider bringing us your next work? Regardless of the genre."

"Of course I will," I lie. I have no intention of writing again.

The remainder of our lunch passes in relative silence. More food passes our lips than words. Small-talk over food that David doesn't seem to enjoy. We say awkwardly forced goodbyes, arranging to exchange emails and organise some festival appearances he already knows I won't agree to.

We leave each other at the top of the stairs outside the Blytheswood Square Hotel. I head along towards West George Street, largely because it's the opposite direction from where David is going. As I turn into West George Street, I clatter face first into the chest of a tall man walking the street at pace. Staggering back, I feel him catch my arm to steady me. His grip is strong but doesn't hurt me. It isn't intended to. It's also familiar. With a smooth strength he pulls me just enough to right me. Only then do I look up at his face.

"Sorry Alice. You alright?" Jim asks.

Despite how we left things when we last spoke, I'm glad to see his face.

"God, Jim. You startled me."

"No easy task," he smiles down at me. He looks well. Happy.

The rush of the last few weeks suddenly catches me in its tailwind. The extra kills, the media attention, my decade-long goal finally in sight. Whatever pressure or joy or fear or excitement recent events have brought suddenly feels a great deal to process. Overwhelming.

Jim narrows his eyes in concern. "What?" he asks.

Something uncharacteristic, a need I've not experienced for a long time washes over me. Suddenly I'd like nothing more than to enclose myself in this good, decent man's arms and cry. Not talk, not ask to be saved, not even to absorb any of his strength to steel me for what's to come; just to cry. I allow my predatory side to assert itself, but only a little, enough to force the need down. Banish it from my consciousness.

"It's nothing, Jim," I say. My voice has already returned to the flat matter-of-fact tone I've used too often with him. Immediately a weariness returns to his eyes.

"Of course it's nothing," he says sadly.

Stood looking into his eyes, this man I've spent hundreds of hours with, embracing, making love with and laughing with, all I see is the hurt he feels that I've kept him so firmly at a distance.

We stand looking at each other for a few very long moments, each of us accepting the norm between us. At least one of us wishes the impasse, the walls, could be breached.

"You look well, Jim," I say, meaning it.

"Thanks Alice. You too," he replies.

Less than two minutes in each other's company and I've already forced his natural warmth to recede. I know that I'm no good for him, I'm not a person anyone needs in their life, but knowing a thing and seeing the effect of it on someone are two very different experiences.

I decide again for an infinitesimally small moment that I want to hold him. More accurately, for him to hold me. From the bar to our right, a young woman emerges and surprises me by moving in behind Jim to wrap her arms around his waist.

Turning in her arms, Jim enfolds her in his own. "Ready to go, Kate?" he asks kindly.

She laughs warmly. She has one of those laughs and one of those smiles, that make you like her immediately. The smile drops when she notices me.

"Oh," Jim reacts. "This is my friend, Alice."

Her wide eyes and slack jaw tell me that she recognises me.

She recovers quicker than most and surprises me by stepping forward to give me a kiss on the cheek. "Lovely to meet you, Alice. My kid is a huge fan of your books."

I thank her. I often practice my grateful face.

As the newly-minted couple turn around the corner into Blytheswood Square, Jim looks back over his shoulder. With a single nod, he bids me goodbye. As they disappear out of sight, his date hiss-whispers too loudly.

"You didn't tell me that you know Alice Connolly," she says, with more volume than she intends. I tune out and I don't hear Jim's reply.

A howling wind prompts me to pull my coat collar more tightly as I descend the long slope towards Queen Street Station, the coldness at my back adding to my pace.

***

It's not a day for bikers. The ground is crisp and frosty, with the odd patch of black ice to keep me sharp. More worrying is the wind, every biker's worst enemy. The trip along the M8 through to Edinburgh has been hairy, but I'm here now. I leave my helmet in place, pull my bike onto its stand and sit upright, feet on the pegs, to stretch my back out and try to put some warmth back into the muscles and bones.

Excitement and wariness war within. Sat in the car park of Morrison's off Ferry Road, I can't help but be overly vigilant. The McKenna home is less than two miles from here. Under normal circumstances, I wouldn't be near a recent kill again so soon, but these are far from normal times. A shiver, that has nothing to do with the nip in the air, vibrates up my spine. This will be my final kill. At least for five years. Maybe forever.

Not for the first time I lose myself in *what ifs* and *what may comes* for several hours, trying to imagine my life without Tequila in it. Even in the short term, it's an uncomfortable thought. Having killed deliberately and regularly for almost a decade, I've maintained a professional detachment to the process of the hunt and the kill. A small part of me is aware that, on some level, I'm undoubtedly enjoying the power and taking the power from the men I've killed. Sure, I focus on the freeing of the spouses, the gift I give them of a new life, but a small part of me fears I'm just like any other addict: making justifications for my actions, allowances for my need to kill.

I dismount my bike, stretching my legs. Resting my rear end on the bike, I prepare for a long wait for Jenny Watson.

I sent Jenny a text as I left Hamilton, directing her to a PO-box outside the supermarket. The usual message.

A new life awaits you if you have the courage to take it.

For the first time, it occurs to me that perhaps Jenny will link my invitation and the contents of the PO box to Tequila's kills. Never before have I been public like this. If she's been watching TV at all she will have heard of my kills. Will she connect the missing women to the note I left for her?

I decide that it's unlikely. The police haven't disclosed, or don't know, what the spouses of my previous kills have done with their lives, where they are, or that they were assisted by me.

The crunch of tyres on the frosted tarmac pulls me from my thoughts. A smile grows on my face as I watch Jenny's little Mini Cooper make its way in a circuitous route around the car park to the PO-boxes. I check my watch. Nine a.m. She's up and about early and has both kids with her, which surprises me as today's a school day. Leaving her kids in the warmth of the running car, she takes furtive looks along the car park as she exits her vehicle. Using the combination I gave her for the PO-box, the door pops open and Jenny checks around her once again, perhaps fearful that her husband may chance by. Unlikely, since although they live nearby he rarely rises before eleven.

My heart races as I watch her reach into the little box and pull out my letter.

Dearest Jenny,

I've watched you struggle, fight and suffer at the hands of your husband. Your dignity and will to survive is immense. Your capacity to endure, staggering. However, the depths of the strength you've accessed to make it this far are not infinite. You will sink under eventually.

Life was not meant to be this way for you. Remember the girl you were, the dreams you had. Try to recall a trace of the desire and ambition you once held before he convinced you that you didn't deserve those things, that you were incapable, that you are less than what you really are.

The will and heart and your capacity for living the life you once envisaged are still there. Snatch onto the threadbare tendrils of who you were and pull them close. You don't have to believe that you can be that person you meant to be, you just have to believe that you can take this new life I've left in this locker for you and make it what you wish it to be. That you can live it, one day at a time, as you see fit.

You do not require anyone's permission to do so. You don't even have to think ahead to what or who or how. You merely have to decide you want to, take the contents of the locker and start over. Right now, this very minute.

You can never return. Your husband will never find you, I will make sure of that for you, and I will punish that man for how he's brought you to his heel; for how he has stripped away at your self-esteem and confidence, to a sliver of what you once possessed.

Believe this: you have the strength, you can be who you were, or you can be anyone else you wish to be free of your abuser. You merely have to choose. Whatever choice you make, I shall of course respect your wishes. Please, take your kids, escape this malicious shadow over your lives.

All my hopes and dreams for you in your new life.
Press In,
Tequila.

Jenny surprises me by straightening her back. At the rear of the car park, partially obscured by a trolley shelter, I watch her, unnoticed. Very few of the spouses I've made my offer to have reacted in the manner Jenny currently is. Her back straight, her jaw clenched in determination, she visibly makes a resolution very quickly, even before checking the contents of the rucksack. Most of the spouses who displayed this reaction simply replaced the contents of the locker, passing on my offer. My heart sinks and I begin mentally sorting through details of the next three potential kills on my list.

Three.

Three I've prepped for thoroughly enough to risk moving onto the next phase. One in Manchester, one in Hull, the last in

Cornwall. Despite my preparations, I simply won't be ready to make an alternative kill for at least seven days.

Weighing the risk of moving one of these kills up the schedule against the need to use the momentum I have with the media at present, I sag a little on deciding that seven days is indeed required. My fist clenches in frustration and disappointment, both at the delay and at Jenny's apparent choice to remain with her abuser.

Mounting my bike again, I notice that Jenny hasn't closed the locker yet and still clutches my letter. Her face is set in grim determination as she returns to the car. Opening the passenger door, she beckons to her ten-year-old daughter, Molly, to move into the rear seat alongside her baby sister, Caitlin.

Once the kids are buckled in again, she returns to the locker to retrieve the rucksack. A cursory glance to confirm its contents and Jenny plonks it onto the recently vacated passenger seat. Resuming her position at the wheel, Jenny skids a little as she tears out of the little car park.

Elated, I grin goofily behind the mask of my helmet and follow her. She surprises me once again, by taking Pilton Drive instead of Ferry Road, which would be a natural route to the airport or bus station.

Christ! She's going home.

I race through a series of panicky scenarios that may play out, or reasons that she may have for returning home. I don't like any of them. Gavin is undoubtedly at home, probably asleep, but what could be important enough for her to return to the family home? She can replace anything left there.

I follow along Pilton Drive, keeping my distance and make the turn into the Strada estate well behind Jenny's Mini. My mind assaults me, practically screaming reasons at me that I shouldn't be here. The estate is littered with CCTV, enough to ensure that my image has already been captured. In normal circumstances, I'd abandon the kill. I may yet have to do so, depending on what plays out when Jenny returns home. Dammit.

I watch from a distance, partially obscured from the cameras under some tree branches, my bike's engine still running. Any hope I harbour that she will make a stealthy run in and out of her house to retrieve some important item disappears as Jenny fetches both girls from the car, grabs the rucksack and enters her home.

What the hell is she doing?

Leaving the Triumph on its stand, I remove my helmet and smooth down the blonde, crop-cut wig beneath before I make my way in what I hope is a casual stroll to stand near the house. I position myself out of direct sight of any of the windows and cock my head, attempting to tune into any sounds from within. Movement in the living room catches my eye. It looks like Jenny is leaving the girls downstairs and is ascending the staircase.

My heart shifts in my chest as I watch her silhouette pass the window in the front door and disappear up to the first floor. Thankfully I recall that I have a camera in the living room and a mic on the upstairs landing and retrieve my white phone from my coat pocket. Opening the software, I locate the Watsons' feeds and hold the phone to my ear, hoping desperately that the mic on the upper hall will pick up any sounds from the bedroom.

Two eternally long minutes' pass during which a thousand dreads flicker through my imagination. As I'm about to switch to the camera feed from the living room, Jenny's voice breaks through.

"Wake up, you piece of shite." Her voice shakes, but not with fear. She's furious. It dawns on me that Jenny has some spirit left, she's come home to get closure. God help her, she has come to tell him she's leaving.

Sounds of Gavin emerging from a drowse shuffle across the audio link. He wakes and as is typical of him, angers quickly. "Who the fuck do you think you're talking to?" he hisses at her.

Jen doesn't bother with preamble. "Fuck you, Gav. I'm leaving . . . me and the kids."

A short period of menacing silence passes and is then broken by Gavin's mocking laughter.

"You're going nowhere," Gavin hisses at her.

A rustle of movement hurts my ear, so intently have I tuned into the sounds coming from the room. The sound of fist on bone that comes next is unmistakable.

My muscles bulge taut and rigid as I try to calm myself and fail. Every instinct is screaming at me to get inside. A decade of discipline roots my feet while I race through my options. If I enter the house, disguise or not, I'm unprepared for a kill. The presence of Jenny and the girls aside, which is enough reason to keep my distance, my kill gear currently sits in my Hamilton apartment. I'm dressed in my own clothes, lacking any of the underclothing I typically employ and my fingertips are bare, aside from my riding gloves. If I enter that house, even for a moment, my DNA will be shed and will sit waiting for any subsequent forensic techs. Bad enough that I may have left blood at a recent kill, this is a whole other level of exposure.

I scan the neighbours' windows quickly. Most of them are in darkness, their occupants having left for their day's activities and responsibilities. The flats facing the houses, though, have many lights present. A couple of the balconies looking down onto the Watson home host dressing-gown wearing smokers getting their first nicotine hit of the day.

Fists clenched tightly enough to turn the skin white, I force myself to remain in place whilst wet thuds from his fists and feet are transmitted over the audio feed.

I can't go in. I can't, I repeat like a mantra. *She'll leave him afterwards and I'll come back for the bastard later.*

Each of the justifications I present to myself for not intervening, for allowing the coward to beat his wife once again, burn like venom in my veins and mind. Two things take the decision from me, Gavin is shouting now and laying into Jenny with an abandon he previously hasn't and Molly is halfway up the staircase responding to the noise.

Another life flashes before my eyes. Another woman, on the floor, being beaten, a sister determined to intervene. Thirty seconds later, thirty very costly indecisive seconds, I'm ten paces at full sprint towards the door to their house before I even realise I'm moving.

26

"It's quite a case you have this time, Kathy," Bobby says before scooping a spoonful of his chocolate ice cream into his mouth.

Kathy's own mouth busy working on her own dessert, she nods her agreement.

It's a lovely restaurant, Italian, family owned, down by the harbour in Newhaven. Bobby's company is easy, as ever, but *as ever* Kathy's attention is elsewhere. Bobby, being Bobby, knows this and is talking through the case with Kathy to help clear her cluttered mind.

He resumes. "So, you have the blog, which really is only useful as an insight into her mind-set and method, but ultimately I can't see it leading you to her."

"Agreed," Kathy replies. "I've messaged her several times now, trying to open a communication line, but she hasn't replied."

Bobby shrugs. "Would you in her position?"

"Probably not," Kathy admits with a resigned smile. "But this type of killer generally does like to communicate in some way, it's like a need for recognition, or simply to explain themselves, even if it's only to tell us how superior they are."

"She *does* communicate and more so than any other serial killer I know of," Bobby points out.

"Yes, but. . ." Kathy's voice trails off and she shoves her unfinished dessert away. "I don't know, Bobby, I just felt that she may talk directly to me, I have no idea why."

Several minutes pass by in the comfortable silence earned after decades of marriage. Neither of them feels the need to fill the empty air. Kathy watches Bobby finish his ice cream, smiling at the fine chocolate moustache he's acquired.

With the last of his dessert finished, something occurs to him. Bobby locks eyes with his wife.

"So just the blood then? That's your only real lead after, what, twenty kills?"

Kathy nods. "The only lead that might help us find her quickly at any rate, but the criminal database hasn't turned up a match. Unless our Tequila has been charged with a crime in the past, she won't be on the database. Seems that is the case."

Making a little scribble gesture on the palm of her hand, Kathy signals the waiter that she'd like the bill.

"My treat tonight, Bobby," she says.

Bobby's eyes light up. "Oh aye?" He waves his hand to catch the waiter before he leaves. "Scuze me, son. Can you bring me a double Glenmorangie and add it to that bill? No ice. Thanks."

Kathy smiles warmly at his opportunistic cheek. "Smart-arse," she accuses.

A few minutes later the couple walk unhurriedly, hands clasped, towards home. Kathy snuggles her neck and the lower part of her face into the folds of Bobby's scarf which she's borrowed. As they begin the ascent up Newhaven Road, Bobby's pace slows, then stops. Turning to Kathy, his brow is furrowed.

"You said *criminal database*. Does that mean there are others?"

"Not really," Kathy replies, her own brow mirroring her husband's. "There's the victims' database, but we generally use that for evidence building, rather than performing criminal searches."

"Got to be worth a search though, right?"

Kathy shakes her head. Ready to argue the pointlessness of searching the victims' database, abruptly her eyes widen. Holding an index finger up to Bobby, she mouths *one minute, love,* whilst speed-dialling the office.

"Gilmour. Do a search and comparison on the victims' DNA database this time, using the blood from the Stevenson scene."

Kathy exchanges a few comments with the young officer then hangs up.

Smiling up at her husband, she says, "Thanks Bobby. I knew if I kept you around long enough, you'd come in handy one day."

Bobby grins broadly and takes her in his arms.

"You must love having such a clever husband."

Kathy reaches up to wipe away his chocolate moustache with a thumb.

"Right you are, genius," she laughs.

Then...

27

Light peeped in through a narrow slit in the shades, piercing my eyes though their lids. Unable to find the will to rise from my bed and close it, or even cover my eyes, I simply rolled my head to the side. Drifting in and out of a restless, purgatory state where I was unsure if I was awake or truly asleep, I became aware of someone in the room. The cadence and weight of his steps told me Seb had returned to read to me once again.

I had no notion of how many days I'd lain in the sterile looking white room, Seb's visits are my only markers of the hours passing. He'd come early in the morning, stay for what I guessed was several hours and leave to return again for a longer spell after the sun had moved away from my window. He read to me, talked of the day's news, chatted about his family – his grown kids and deceased wife. His time in the Marines came up often and always carried along a sense of regret. In hindsight, he may have been the only thing keeping me sane.

Today felt different. I felt a little increase in my focus, a fraction more able than before. Perhaps the painkillers' dose had been reduced, perhaps the antibiotics in my IV were finally beating my infection back. Whatever had caused the change, I was regaining something of myself.

I opened my eyes a minute amount that the light wouldn't hurt. Seb was sat in a comfortable chair, the type one only finds in hospitals at bedsides. One leg crossed loosely over the other, he scanned his newspaper for stories to share. Observing him in silence for several moments, I noted a tall, powerful-looking man, with quick eyes, clever hands and a gentle manner that belied his physicality.

My voice a dry, disused, barely audible croak, Seb still jumped out of his skin when I said his name aloud.

"Alice," he stammered. Relief and surprised vied for dominance. "You startled me."

Seb placed a hand on my cheek. His gesture and easy familiarity soothed my aching spirit. "You feel much cooler," he said. "Almost normal."

"How long have I been here?"

Sadness filled his eyes. "Almost an entire week," he said. "You were very ill, Alice. You had an infection in your uterus from the . . ." His voice trailed off.

I nodded that he should continue.

"Well, you know. They've had you on several antibiotics. Actually they were considering trying a more powerful one later today, so it's good to see your fever breaking."

"What else?" I demanded.

Seb's eyes shifted away from me. He looked like he wanted to fetch someone, anyone.

"Seb?" I prompted.

He sighed deeply. "Your uterus and cervix were infected, badly. Some material left inside had caused a massive infection in your reproductive organs which then became systemic. They had to operate. They had to remove your uterus and your ovaries. I'm really sorry, Alice."

I hadn't thought there was this much pain in the world. Recent experiences should've taught me differently.

Stoically, I nodded firmly once.

"Look, I was gonna go get something to eat. Let me fetch a doctor and I'll come back later. We'll talk properly, once you've had a chance to process. Kay?"

***

Detached, I listened to the doctor explain the procedures they'd performed on me, the likely implications of their actions and the expectation for my recovery. Her words registered in my consciousness and I even managed the occasional reply, but I simply didn't dedicate any surface thoughts to what she was *discussing* with me. I had bigger concerns. I had plans to make and I had so very much to learn.

Sensing that the doctor was awaiting a reply, I tuned back into her presence.

"I'm sorry, could you repeat that last part again?"

Smiling patiently, she repeated, "We hope to discharge you within a few days, Alice, if your white blood cell levels continue to improve."

"Thanks, Doctor," I managed, turning away from her once again to focus on a spot on the wall and resume my planning.

***

"Can I help you with that, Alice?"

Having dressed before he'd come back into the room, I was now exhausted and unable to summon the mental strength to lean over and tie my shoes.

"Yes please," I conceded.

On one knee, Seb tied my laces with patient consideration. A moment's reflection and he double-bowed them. "In case they loosen and you trip."

A memory of my sister tying my laces in the same manner threatened to surface. Shoving it roughly aside, I thanked Seb coldly. He rose to his feet, his expression less affable. "Are you sure you're ready to leave," he asked.

I bobbed my head in reply, whilst I zipped my bag closed and searched for levity.

"C'mon," I told him, forcing a smile. "I could kill for a burger."

***

"Yes, but is it possible?" I asked Seb for maybe the third time.

Almost concealing a grimace this time, he sucked air in through his teeth before replying.

"Possible, yeah. Advisable. . . no."

Unable and unwilling to mask my rising irk, I lifted my eyebrows, challenging him to elaborate.

"Alice, it's been a month. Don't get me wrong, you've recovered well, but you still have a long way to go physically." Seb's eyes broke contact with my own. "Mentally. . . well, I just can't know."

Flicking his eyes back to mine, sympathy and concern emanated from him.

"Alice, what you've been through. . . you've endured so much. I'm not saying that you don't have the right, or that you don't possess the commitment to do as you plan to, but is the need really there?"

I motioned for him to continue.

"You have plenty of money in the bank, millions thanks to your sis. . . to your time as an investment banker. You have a new identity, the means to completely restart your life, be anyone you choose. Is this really who you wish to be?"

Allowing the mild anger I was experiencing to dissipate, I looked at Seb for several long seconds before speaking.

His fondness for me was plain; his decency evident in his deeds and words. This man had taken me in, mended me, restored the resources I'd need and simply cared for me when I couldn't fall any further. Despite this, he still didn't have any real intimation, no idea, about who and what I now was.

Softening my voice, I leaned in as I spoke to him.

"Seb, the things I've endured are exactly what compels me to proceed as planned. The need to atone, to punish I suppose, comes from that same survival. I do, I need to and I need your help, at least to begin."

I observed a stream of arguments cross his mind in his expression. Finally, his face showed merely resignation.

"Alright Alice. Let's go over it again, shall we?"

Placing my hand over his, I fought back welling tears.

"Thank you."

Seb nodded stiffly. Moving his attention to his notes, he recapped the details of our long discussion.

"Okay, this guy here," Seb pointed at a name I already knew by heart. "Firearms. These three, Krav Maga, field first-aid and surveillance." Seb glanced up at me to check I was listening. "Over in New York, this guy is blades and tactics. In Colorado, we have a tech guy to tutor you. After that, we'll reassess. That okay?"

I nodded once.

"Alright then, Alice," he said, his voice strengthening. "One more month first though, just until you're well enough."

I moved to argue and found myself silenced by his raised finger.

"One month of recovery and light core work, or no access to my contacts," he said bluntly.

"Deal."

Now...

28

Clattering through the unlocked door, I take in the living room as I pass at pace. The baby is asleep in her car seat, blissfully unaware of the violence in her home. She's probably had the sounds of abuse as the soundtrack to her short life so pays no mind.

A blur, I ascend the stairs. Cutting a right at the top, I fall to my knees, a string-less marionette, at the sight of the room before me.

Jenny's face is no longer. In its place rests an unidentifiable tangle of slender meat and gristle, slick with dark blood and imprinted with the shape of her husband's fists. Her hair covers half of her former face, for this I'm selfishly grateful. I'm too late for her, I failed her.

Anger, shock and disbelief at the damage he's done to her, mingled with a tide of long-buried memories, weigh me down and immobilise my frame, leaving me crouched on all fours staring into the room. I blink my eyes dumbly several times attempting to make the events unfolding in front of them change somehow.

Gavin has his hands around his daughter's throat. He has squeezed her so hard her face and eyes bulge. Her neck sits at an unnatural angle. Still he grips and squeezes, determined to end her. At that moment, I hate myself for the rigidity of my shock. Practiced as I am, I quickly push back at the rising fear, allowing my cold predator to the fore.

An instant later I race towards him unheeded. So intent is this pathetic, bestial man on throttling his eldest child, I don't register in his world.

My foot connects with speed and savage power. A vicious front kick he's unprepared for snaps his head around, dislocating his jaw and sending him sprawling onto his back.

I don't have time to punish Watson, I just need to end him. Ignoring the urge to help Molly, I continue my run, launching myself a short distance through the air to land with a knee pinning his left arm, the other pressing down into his windpipe.

He tries to scream in rage but can't open his jaw. The attempt forces any air he had in his lungs out and I lean harder onto his throat, feeling the cartilage begin to give slightly.

Watson isn't a big man, abusers rarely are, but he has power in his muscles and his punches are well-practiced. Pushing past the pain, asphyxiation and fading consciousness, he rides the adrenaline and pumps his fist into my side several times. A rasping choke comes from Molly beside us. Despite my leather riding jacket, the ferocity of Watson's blows drives the air from me. I choke in a lungful of iron-tinged air and press harder with both knees. The cartilage in his windpipe snaps wetly and his eyes start to roll upwards. I risk a glance at Molly. Her eyes meet mine, pleading with me to help her. With one final, hateful punch Gavin breaks one of my ribs and then loses consciousness. I keep the pressure on until he's dead.

I crawl towards the kid, holding my side. She's silent now, still. No breath escapes her lips or nose. Her chest does not rise or fall. The kid's eyes are still bulged open. Her neck is already darkening, the coming bruises shaped for her father's hands.

I yell inwardly at my rising panic. *Not now!*

On the dresser to my right I find an opportunity in the form of a Bic pen. I remove my gloves and feel for her Adam's apple, then stroke down until I feel the cricoid cartilage. Stroking back up towards the Adam's apple, I confirm the indentation I'm searching for and shove the point of the pen into the soft tissue. Withdrawing the pen, I dismantle it in under a second, grasping tightly to the hollow plastic tube, discarding the rest.

With a pinch I open the puncture wound and place my finger inside the slit to open it. Delicately I slide the pen tube a few centimetres into the space I've created. With no hesitation, I breathe into the tube with two quick breaths, pause for five seconds and then give one more breath. Her lungs inflate and her chest rises. After a few chest compressions, I return to blowing into the tube. Each time I alternate, her chest rises a little less. Her breastplate and ribs give under the force of my chest compressions. Still I cannot accept that this sweet young kid is gone.

After a period of time that feels like both an eternity and a spilt second, I collapse onto my back beside her. My muscles won't stop trembling. My vision is blurring, I'm drenched in sweat. All I can think is how it's my fault, all of it. Memories of my sister and another of my many lives surge once again.

I lie aside their bodies for a long time. In automatic pilot my brain shuts out what's around me. The dead child, her mother by her side, maimed and murdered, both.

Falling back on the complex logistics of maintaining a life like mine to remove the growing press of old memories, I focus on the task in front of me. Robotically, I remove my consciousness from their torn world and begin mentally listing the evidence the police will find in this house.

Fingerprints, plenty of skin cells, my mucus on the pen and most likely hair, as my wig has fallen off. They'll check the CCTV and see me on my bike coming and going from the Watson home. It's a good thing I'm prepared. I smile humourlessly, feeling hollow at my cleverness.

I lie there, coaching myself to breathe deeply, in through the nose, out through the mouth, filling breaths from the diaphragm. The process of shutting myself off from that which I can't cope with surprises and pleases me by beginning automatically. I hadn't thought I was capable of processing these raw emotions any more. I've been so single-minded, so sure, so clinical for so very long.

My psyche shields itself by forcing my usual cool logic to wash over my thoughts.

The relief is immense. I don't want to feel for these people. I will not. An instant later my resolve is destroyed by the cry of an infant.

Failure presses on me heavily. I want to scream. I want nothing more than to lie here and lose myself in the ruin of these people's lives. I want with all my soul to thrash and cry and rail until the police come for me. Another cry splits my world and puts my wants into a distant second place. With monumental effort, I rise, carrying all the guilt and pain my brain tried to protect me from. I heft the weight of it, curse it and make my way toward Caitlin's cries on shaky legs.

29

"What a fucking mess," Steve states without humour for the third time since they began poring over the Kinney case files.

Sitting with legs crossed on the floor, Buddha-style, surrounded by folders and files, Gilmour looks up at the sergeant. "Sir," he agrees.

Kathy pins another length of red string to the board, stretches it between two documents and ties it off.

"Let's start building a picture then," she says. "Bring me what you have for the board."

Since identifying the blood found at the Stevenson kill as belonging to a Bellshill woman named Nicole Kinney, the team have spent almost eight hours searching through details and evidence from the historic case. Decades old, most of the evidence is held on mouldered and dusty files. Steve has been complaining incessantly about the effect on his lungs. Gilmour, a child of the twenty-first century, a data-bred millennial, wears a disdainful expression. Kathy is in her element. The feel of physical files and bags of evidence is familiar and reassuring.

Nicole Kinney died in her Lanarkshire home at twenty-four years of age. Pregnant, young, a promising writer, the girl's death was brutal and had been attributed to her older sister, Alice Kinney. Nicole's long-term boyfriend, Darren Houston, was also found dead in their home. Both bodies showed signs of having been beaten by a blunt item, most likely a fist. The altercation had been severe enough to cause greenstick fractures in several bones of both victims. Darren's eye socket had been broken and a dent in the rear of his skull suggested that he'd been hit with a heavy object and most likely rendered unconscious before he died.

Nicole had been strangled to death.

Their home had been set to flames, the Fire Department reporting that a petrol-based accelerant was used. Forensics were able to retrieve DNA from both victims by drilling through the burnt bones to extract the bone marrow.

Nicole's DNA was matched by cross-referencing with her father's, a man who had been estranged from his daughters for years after they were removed from the family home and taken into care. The DNA he donated which confirmed his daughter's death was probably the most useful thing he'd ever done for the kid.

He had since died.

The investigating officers logged evidence that Alice had flown in from her home in San Francisco two days previously to visit her sister. The night of the murder, whilst fire fighters doused the flames on Nicole's home and body, Alice Kinney returned to the States on a red-eye flight. Once in San Francisco, she disappeared. She was, to date, the only suspect on the double murder and was presumed to be the killer.

Despite extensive enquiries and a monumental effort from the SFPD and even the FBI, Alice had never been traced. A woman with means, a millionaire investment banker, Alice certainly had the funds available to vanish in a country as varied and huge as America.

Kathy steps aside to observe from a distance as Steve and Gilmour take turns to add to and make connections on the investigation board. As they place photos, reports and travel records relating to the case, the Chief Superintendent slips into the room.

"Don't let me interrupt, just here to observe," McBride says holding a hand up.

Kathy gives him a tight nod and turns back to scan the emerging connections between the facets of the Kinney case. Steve and Gilmour complete their tasks, Steve mumbling something to himself absent-mindedly as he pins the last of the travel records for Alice Kinney to the board.

The Super coughs, clearing his throat. "I remember this case," he says conversationally. "I was based in Lanarkshire, Hamilton actually, at the time, a short secondment during my time here as DI." McBride turned to face Kathy. "Remember?"

Kathy nods in the affirmative. The office had been unbearable for the spell McBride had been away. She remembered it well.

McBride returned his attention to the case board.

"My Bellshill and Motherwell colleagues worked very hard to find the sister to no avail. Terrible waste of a young couple's lives. Twenty-something, weren't they?"

"Yes," Kathy confirms.

"Hmm. Nasty stuff," the Super asserts.

Kathy nods in reply, returning her eyes to the board. Following lines of string, she tries for a new perspective on the facts. Nothing is forthcoming. The case has been closed for years, aside from an arrest warrant for Alice Kinney dating back twenty years or so. The Super shifts noisily, fidgeting in his seat, distracting her. She forces herself to resist admonishing her superior for his distracting presence at such a crucial time.

Clearing his throat once again, the Super leaves his seat to approach the board. Kathy can't prevent an exasperated sigh from escaping as he blocks her view.

The Super appears not to notice as he peers in for a closer look at the travel records of Alice Kinney.

Steve notes Kathy's irritation and steps between them before she says something she'll regret.

"Can I help with something, sir?" he asks, voice jovial.

A few quiet seconds pass without reply.

"Sir?" Steve asks again, more forcefully.

The Super's head whips around. "Oh, sorry, Steve, Kathy. . . it's just that there's something tickling at my memory about this particular aspect."

The Super points out several items, including the travel records. Kathy forces herself to relax and reminds herself that the Super was once a detective and a good one. Backing off, the team give their boss the space and time to enter that zone good investigators slip into where the world around them ceases to exist and they can mentally immerse themselves in a case. The Super stands, visualising, backtracking, sorting through decades of experiences. He's searching his memory, connecting events, names, faces, reports that've crossed his desk, anything really that pertains to this case he had such minimal exposure to at the time of the investigation. The Super stays very still for a long time, the only signs of movementa tapping of the middle finger of his right hand against its palm, and his eyes scanning across the board.

His head finally lifts and his back straightens.

"Do you have any files from a Jack Blythe?"

"Aye," Steve replies instantly. "There's one in the associated case files. Hang on."

Steve moves to a small stack of folders sat away from the main investigation boxes and files. After a moment's sorting, he returns with a yellowed manila folder. The Super accepts it with a nod of thanks. Without explanation, he begins flipping through the contents of the file, mumbling to himself as he discounts certain pages over others, which are moved to the top. When he's content that he has assembled the information he needs, he removes five pages from the top of the file, discarding the remainder of the folder.

"Come look at these," he invites his detectives.

Forming around the Super, Kathy, Gilmour and Steve crane their necks in to scan the files and photos as their boss talks them through his thoughts.

"Around five years after the Kinney case had been archived, a junior detective, Blythe, sought permission from me to investigate a hunch he had." The Super spreads five files across the desk to his left. "Blythe had made the Kinney case something of a hobby. Ultimately, he didn't have much luck, but I recall that Alice Kinney's travel to the States in particular intrigued him."

Running his finger across the files laid out, the Super continues. "Blythe compiled a list of women who had entered the UK from the States and subsequently did not leave. He chose a two-year window after the Kinney couple died and listed every woman he could trace. Blythe then applied several criteria – age, height and build, previous travel to and from the UK – to eliminate around four hundred women. These five are who he was left with."

Her eyebrows rising in hopeful surprise, Kathy asks, "Blythe thought that Alice had returned to the UK under another identity? Did he follow through on any of them?"

The Super shook his head. "No. Blythe emigrated to New Zealand not long after he filed those reports. Seems his hobby remained just that. These were never followed up on."

Steve nods along. "Not surprising, though. Most likely these were initially submitted with a stack of other unrelated cases and reports that Blythe would have been required to return as he was leaving the force."

"Yes," the Super confirms. "I expect this file made its way into the Kinney files without anyone looking past the label."

The team take a step back, as though the distance will give them a new perspective.

"If he's correct," Kathy says softly, "if one of these women is Alice Kinney then the blood we found at Stevenson's is likely hers."

Gilmour nods his agreement. "Nicole was confirmed dead using the DNA found in her bone marrow via comparison with her father's, but it's possible that Nicole's archived DNA that we matched to our Stevenson sample was simply a near match, rather than a perfect one. It could easily be Alice Kinney's blood. It's possible that as siblings they share enough markers to cause a match on the sample. These tests only analyse a small percentage of a person's DNA at any rate. It wouldn't be the first false match we've had, not by a long way."

The room remains silent for what feels like a very long time. Eventually Steve snorts in laughter.

"Good on ye, Chief," he blurts. McBride smiles wryly.

Gilmour laughs nervously.

"Let's check these addresses and start tracing these women," Kathy says.

Then...

30

Salt, iron-scented blood and sweat stung my eyes. I blinked hard to expel enough of the fluid to clear my vision.

"Again," Scranton barked.

Whipping my head to the side violently, I shook the running fluids from my forehead and lunged forward once again.

"You locked your elbow. You failed to tilt at the wrist at the moment of the strike."

Scranton paced at my side, his disapproval filling the room as much as the metallic vapour from the corpse. "Again."

Fifteen more minutes passed in this manner. Added to the twenty I'd already spent failing at his technique, the additional time allocated caused two things. My strikes, whilst weaker, started to become more focused. Cleaner, precise, unstoppably perfect. My muscles also gained an insidious tremor with the prolonged exertion.

"Enough," he said, nodding at the barrel of ice-water in the rear of the basement room. The heavy butcher blade dropped from my loose grasp to clang on the white tiled floor. For the first time, I sank my arms into the painful stab of the water with gratitude. Almost instantly the tremors stopped. The muscles tightened and then began to shake uncontrollably, with the cold this time.

"Switch."

Without looking at him, I removed my arms from the ice-water barrel, transferring them to a large sink filled with very warm water. I almost passed out as the raw tingling made its way along the length of my arms. My muscles practically flopped in relief. "Switch."

I moved between barrels for five minutes. Alternating between curing freeze and comforting heat, I lost all sense of sensation in my arms. In a state of submissive obedience, I paid attention only to what I was experiencing, but refused to feel the pain. He snapped me from my robotic routine as I pulled my arms from the warmth.

"Rest," he said calmly, handing me a mug of ginger tea to fortify and revive me.

Knowing the quarter he'd given me would be brief, I drank quickly. The pig carcass I'd been stabbing was a shredded mess on the concrete floor. Its fluids ran in long rivulets towards the floor drain in the centre of the room.

Before I'd emptied the mug, we resumed.

Scranton slid a fresh pig corpse along. Suspended from hook and chain, it swung merrily, inviting me to my task.

"Precision work," Scranton announced, handing me a smaller, more refined blade with a wicked point and razor edge.

"Aorta. . . femoral. . . carotid. . . radial."

Whilst Scranton called out targets, I moved around the suspended pig. At times I made stealthy strikes; occasionally I performed a brutal lunge-stab. At my finest moments I almost caressed the skin, muscle and blood vessel with my blade as I opened it.

The pig oozed slow, dead blood as I danced around it, selecting my targets, changing grip, ferocity and finesse to suit the required strike and angle.

Scranton changed to organs, directing me through kidney, liver, lung and heart strikes, before demanding specific sections of the heart as targets. Once again, I lost myself in the process, becoming merely a body and a blade. . . a macabre instrument.

"Enough," he barked eventually.

His eyes and fingers moved over the precise, neat wounds I'd made in the pig's body. His head nodded once in approval. In the three months I'd spent in his compound, it was the single moment of praise I had received or would again in the weeks to come.

Adrenaline rushed in response to this meagre approval. Pride and resentment battled within me.

Scranton, as always, seemed oblivious to my mental state and was already headed back upstairs.

"We're done for today," he tossed the words over his shoulder.

For a long time, I stood there, arm and blade hanging loosely at my side, caught in a maelstrom of hate, pride and determination. Scranton would give me these breaks from time to time, only to rouse me within the hour to practice or hone some other skill or technique. I wanted so desperately to sleep, but burned with a desire to deny him the satisfaction of waking me cruelly once I'd passed into blissful rest.

A bitter smile pulled at the corner of my lips.

Fuck you, Scranton.

Stepping back into ready position, I raised my blade hand, gave the pig a kick to send it swinging on its hook, then began selecting my own targets.

When Scranton returned he showed no surprise at my having continued the session alone, nor did he show me any further quarter for my efforts. Riding a surge of accomplishment and adrenaline, the denial of a rest period suited me just fine.

As he entered the blood-spattered basement, I stood, drenched in sweat and pig parts, welcoming him with intense abandon. A wiry, leanly-muscled man in his mid-fifties followed Scranton down into the basement.

"Time to graduate from pigs," Scranton said, expressionless.

"Let's get on with it," I demanded coldly.

31

Six months later. . .

The smell of the hallway leading to the detectives' offices brought a strange flush of memories before Kathy's mind's-eye. Most of them negative. Her breath and heart quickened in response. Turning to check on her slowed progress, Steve's eyes filled with sympathy as he noted her apprehensive expression.

"You alright, Kathy?"

Straightening her back, Kathy nodded. "Aye. C'mon, Steve. Let's get this over with."

Steve turned his back to the office doors. Approaching his partner, he placed a hand on her right shoulder.

"It won't be like before, Kathy. Things have changed." His smile emanated reassurance.

"With you perhaps, but there are half a dozen other detectives in there who don't see things the way you do." Kathy's chin lowered to meet her chest.

"Kathy, get a grip. So what if anyone's got anything to say to you? Deal with it like you always do. Make them feel like a chastised schoolchild." Steve grinned, eliciting a spark of humour in Kathy's eyes. "You'll be fine, Kathy. Besides, I told you already, things have changed."

Furrowing her brow, Kathy responded, "Yeah, if you say so."

Laughing outright this time, Steve pulled her into a loose, manly one-armed hug.

"Seriously, Kathy, you should hear the stories that are going around the department. '*McGuire took on three men with knives. . . After she got stabbed she pulled the knife out and shoved it up one guy's ribcage. . . Stabbed six times and kept going. Three months pregnant and still kicked their arses. . .'"*

Kathy let a loud laugh loose.

"You're joking?" she exclaimed. "Who said I was pregnant?"

"That's what you focus on?" Steve laughed. "Look, Kath, you're a fuckin' hero to these men now. They speak about you with a mixture of awe and fear."

Kathy nodded along, feigning a confidence she was only just rediscovering.

"Let's not disappoint them then, Steve," she said, pushing open the double doors.

Inside, welcome home banners, balloons, and cheap wine and cakes greeted her. One large cake had been fashioned with an image of Kathy looking bad-ass in icing. Bearing the legend 'Don't Fuck with McGuire', it made Kathy laugh at the sight. Each of her colleagues turned to welcome her. Smiling, eyes wide, they approached her in a wave. Hands patted her shoulder tentatively. A few shook hands or even embraced her. Most of them wore expressions that were an odd mixture of relief and pride.

All doubt, resentment, fear and guilt left Kathy at that moment. Triumphantly, her old self reasserted itself. Stepping into the midst of the office and her colleagues, Kathy shed the skin of her previous life and embraced the one she'd worked so hard for.

Perhaps an hour had passed, during which Kathy had been passed around the detectives, each of them eager to hear of her experience first-hand. Her status had shifted irrevocably. Even the most hostile of her colleagues had welcomed her back eagerly. They looked upon her with new eyes, regarding her now as capable, one of them.

Steve called for quiet in the room. Raising his half-full glass, he spoke softly. "To Craig Graham."

"To Craig Graham," the room responded.

Steve downed the remains of his glass.

"Right, troops, back to work," he said.

One by one, they trickled back to their desks at Steve's order.

"Not you, Kathy," Steve said. "We're going on a wee trip."

Katy jutted her chin questioningly. Steve was already grabbing his coat and headed to the exit.

***

Despite Steve having stopped at a florist and purchasing a spray of spring flowers, it hadn't dawned on Kathy where they might be going until Steve pulled the car into the gates of Corstorphine Hill Cemetery.

Silently, Kathy leaned over to place a hand over Steve's, who tightened a finger around her thumb in acknowledgment. It felt odd that Steve had chosen to share this aspect of his life with her. Odd, but also comforting that he'd decided to trust her with something so private to him.

Crunching the car to a halt on the red-stoned driveway, Steve exited the car and made his way to a nearby grave. Kathy followed at a respectful distance.

The black stone, shining amongst its much older, weather-beaten neighbours, bore the name of his late wife: Margaret Louise Jackson. Kathy had known that Steve had lost his wife, all the department did, but Steve never talked of her, leading no-one else to mention her either.

Watching Steve lay the flowers carefully against Margaret's gravestone Kathy kept very still despite her discomfort. She couldn't see Steve's face, but his body language had taken on an unfamiliar gait. Leaning in, he kissed his fingertips and left it on Margaret's gravestone.

Minutes stretched as he stood considering, or communing, Kathy didn't know which.

"Five years now," he said suddenly, causing Kathy to start. "Five years. . . she was only twenty-eight, Kathy."

Kathy closed the paces between them, looping her arm through his. At moments like this, good detectives, good friends also, ignored the pushing questions and merely allowed a silence to exist which the other might fill if so inclined.

"Cancer," Steve said flatly. "She was diagnosed in March, dead by the end of April."

Kathy held his arm a little tighter.

"She was beautiful, Kathy. Not just on the outside. She was one of those people that other folk just seem to gravitate to. She was so vital, so full of ideas and plans and love. She was like a balloon you had to cling onto to stop a quick wind lifting her away. Maggie found joy everywhere she looked. She saw goodness and beauty in everyone. . . Even me."

Steve closed his eyes. Remaining still for some time, he eventually broke his moment.

"Can you imagine losing a force of nature like her from your life?"

He didn't really expect an answer. Kathy shook her head anyway.

"It's like all the colour suddenly left the world. Everything became muted, washed out. Like everything I ever believed in, or worked for, or aspired to was just gone. . . Worse, it's like it never existed. Losing Maggie destroyed my world, Kathy. I couldn't open myself up to that kind of hurt again. That's why I've been. . . y'know, such a dick these last few years. I didn't want to care about anyone again and I didn't want anyone to care about me."

"Well, you have Bobby and me now," she said kindly.

Steve merely nodded.

"Maggie would've liked you, Kathy. And you would have loved her."

Steve looked off into the distance as though visualising an alternate world for them.

Breaking off, he regarded Kathy with faraway eyes. "I'm gonna stay here for a while, you can go if you want." His tone made it clear that he wanted her to stay.

Kathy leaned her head against his shoulder. Clinging tightly to her friend's arm, she lent him some of her revived strength.

"I'll stay where I am, partner."

Now...

32

Pain lances my side, my broken rib punishing me with each step. Clenching my jaw against the pain, I make it smaller in my mind, focus on the baby's cries and descend the seemingly never-ending staircase.

Little Caitlin is crying loudly, but her cries are not provoked by fear or in response to the morning's violence. There are no tears; she simply needs attention and this is how she communicates.

Coming down onto my knees, I smile tightly, forcing a gentleness into my voice at odds with the moment. The pain in my ribcage intensifies in protest. Caitlin's cries build as I near her. I push past the notion that I'm scaring the kid. She's just letting me know she needs something, children this young don't generally fear strangers, particularly if they are gentle.

Unbuckling her with clumsy fingers from the car seat, which her struggle has sent rocking, I make shushing noises and say gentle hellos as I lift her. My body reminds me it is broken and pain needles my nervous system. Caitlin's eyes are wide and fixed on me. She notices me grimace tightly in response to the pain in my side and begins screaming again. Finally stood, Caitlin in my arms, I find the breath to comfort her once again.

Every instinct, every raw nerve ending is screaming at me. *Get out of here.*

Anyone could've seen me, could've heard the sounds of violence and heard the baby's cries, but for the moment I just can't care. Caitlin is my entire focus.

Laying her onto the waist-high changing station, I whisper a thank you for the convenience of the platform. My hands work smoothly and gently with haste. Cooing at Caitlin, I remove the wet nappy that's been an irritation to her. She likes me rubbing her feet and rewards me with a smile. By the time I enclose her bottom in a clean nappy and begin redressing her, she's listening to me quietly sing a lullaby I thought I'd forgotten.

On the outside, I wear a conciliatory smile, but internally my mind's racing through a seemingly endless series of options. A growing storm of *what ifs* and *hows* builds momentum. My internal dialogue becomes an undecipherable cacophony.

Caitlin breaks the maelstrom by reaching out to take my index finger, closing her little hand around it. At this very ordinary, simply gesture, something shatters in me, silencing the frantic bombardment.

My heart lurches in my chest. Caitlin throws me a gummy grin as I lift her, bringing her into my arms. She rests her cheek against my breast, taking comfort from the contact. Fearful of breaking the moment, I stay there smelling the top of her head for so long, I begin to wonder if she's fallen asleep. I don't recall having experienced such a moment of peace before. My mind is silent. I'm truly present. Only Caitlin and I exist at that moment.

The reality of the world washes over me once again, but gently this time. What had been a tsunami of fears and thoughts and worries is now simply a choice of paths to select from. Caitlin remains snuggled into my chest as I move around the room and the kitchen retrieving items she'll need. I pack them into a changing bag, prepare her a bottle of milk and gently lower her back into her car seat. Fast asleep, she gives a little startled lurch at the break in contact, but does not wake. I slip the teat of her bottle into her mouth and marvel at how, even asleep, her little hands and mouth work together to keep the bottle in place and the milk flowing.

With Caitlin settled, I turn my mind coldly to assess what action to take. I should leave, take the bike, call the police and direct them to the house. Ultimately it doesn't matter that I've left so much of myself in this place, I've prepared for that. Traffic is light at this time of the morning. I could be in Lanarkshire in under an hour, ditch the bike, probably burn it, get back to my Hamilton apartment and contact Seb to activate my exit strategy.

My eyes narrow and mist. Caitlin has no one left in her family. Both sets of grandparents are dead. There are no aunties or cousins to take her in. Everyone who loves her lies dead upstairs. She would be in the system, in care within hours. The part of me that has already become attached to this child by a fledgling, but powerful bond, fine as spider silk, throbs at the thought of abandoning her.

With a tight nod to myself, I make my choice and exit to the hallway, removing my biker gear as I go, leaving only jeans and a long-sleeve T. Retrieving the pram frame which Caitlin's seat attaches to, I lift her smoothly, like I'm handling explosives and click her seat into place. She sucks more slowly at the milk now, her closed eyes and facial expression the very image of bliss. Every need fulfilled, she is content.

I steal a few minutes to nip outside and wipe down the obvious surfaces on my bike. It's practically a futile gesture, but one borne of habit.

Hanging her changing bag from the pram handle, I wrap the baby well in a travel blanket and take her from her home without regret. Before turning her pram onto Pilton Drive I take a last look at my Triumph. There are few things I'll regret leaving behind in Alice Connolly's life, the bike is one of them.

A short bus ride to Haymarket Station and I'll purchase tickets for several destinations before heading to Glasgow. I'll ditch the wig and the pram, and change my appearance as much as circumstances allow whilst I'm in Waverley Station. Once in Glasgow, I have resources available to me in a storage room in the city centre. And then home. At least for a while.

***

Caitlin yawns lazily, star fishing her arms and legs before curling back into a foetal ball, her cheek pressed into my side. The codeine has finally kicked in, allowing me to drowse in bed beside her.

Deep satisfaction permeates every part of me. This little girl has brought me a sense of peace and of clarity I hadn't known I'd been lacking.

The mid-morning sun slices through a crack in the curtains, cutting across the floor and up onto the bed to warm my toes. I worry that the light may wake her, but laugh at the notion as she slaps at her own face, tending to an itch perhaps and remains sound asleep.

She's such a content little girl. Idly I wonder how many times she's had to comfort herself or sleep through domestic storms despite her mother's care. Having spent the night together, her asleep, me up and down all night, the smell and feel of this baby is as familiar to me as though she'd been in my life for years.

The little mannerisms of sleep enchant me, opening a flood of emotions alien to me for so long. Twelve hours in my life and I belong completely to this angelic, blonde-haired wonder.

Still. . . the world will not simply step back and allow us our new relationship, not without assistance.

Reluctantly, I slip silently from our nest, headed to the living room and my white phone. Checking the time on my phone, I calculate that it's around two a.m. in San Francisco. Seb is likely asleep, but won't grumble at being roused. The small fortune I pay for his services aside, he's my oldest friend and aware of the urgency to my work.

As the phone rings with an international tone, I crane my neck and smile to see Caitlin once again spread languidly across my bed. Seb picks up on the fourth ring. Not asleep after all.

"Hey, Alice," he answers cheerily. "What can I help you with, kiddo?"

"Hi Seb. It's a big job this time, I'm afraid."

"Not a problem. What are we looking at?"

I take a deep breath before replying. "I need you to activate the Terminus Protocol."

An uncharacteristic silence from Seb tells me that he's already on the move.

A moment later, he returns to the phone. "I have the instructions right here," he says. His voice is much flatter than a moment ago. "You sure about this one, kid?" he asks, concern evident.

Without hesitation I confirm that I am and explain that, in addition to the prearranged series of jobs he already has on his plate, I'll be needing adoption papers and a passport for a one-year-old girl.

He resists the urge to enquire after the baby.

"Okay, Alice. It'll take around three hours. I suggest you pack up and book into a hotel. Cash only. Keep your white phone for now, but once I process this, you have to get rid of it, okay?"

"Thanks Seb. Call me when you're done?"

"Course I will, Alice. Stay safe."

Laying my phone on the kitchen counter, I busy myself with making a pot of coffee. I'm going to need the caffeine today. Seb sounded shocked that I asked for the protocol to be activated. I suppose almost ten years have passed since we planned my exit strategy and laid the groundwork so it's only natural that he is a little taken aback.

As I work, my mind shuffles through the arrangements Seb is making for me.

New passport, driving licence and bank accounts, work and credit history, even a decade-old social media profile. A clean identity, again.

Alice Connolly will write an open letter to the media stating her withdrawal from public life. She'll also draft separate confidential instructions to her publishers and agents. All assets and future royalties will be discretely channelled from Alice Connolly's account to a dozen accounts belonging to ghosts. After that they'll be bounced to the account of whoever I'll be by then. My only request to Seb was that I retain a British passport in my new guise. As before, the only reminder of my current life I'll take forward is my Christian name. . . and, of course, this time there will be Caitlin, but she'll never know any life but the one we make together.

I *will* hold those with the power accountable after their five years' grace is over, but perhaps in a different manner than I had intended to. For now, Caitlin is what matters.

All of the lives I've changed and taken. The spouses I've rescued and set free into the world. The children I've removed from abusive homes and parents who don't deserve them. The global discussion I've awoken. All of these things matter more than I can express, but laid next to Caitlin's need, my accomplishments are insignificant and the abused will have to fend for themselves for a while.

I have the opportunity to help this kid become whatever, whoever she chooses to be. To help her become a strong woman, unafraid to move with grace and purpose through this rotten world.

I can be a mother.

I feel bathed in sunlight. Energised, awake and with a purpose that eclipses my former role. Tequila's voice is now small, a whisper under a hurricane where once it had been the eye of that storm. Smiling, I turn to gaze through the doorway into the bedroom once again. Caitlin sticks a little thumb into her mouth and purses her lips around it.

From the corner of my eye I see a silhouette move past the frosted glass of the door to my apartment. It's a woman. She comes to a stop to the left of my door, facing in. A man soon joins her, his larger frame blocking most of the light from the hallway.

Hope dies in me at that instant. I can see the outline of their uniforms in their shadows. I fix my eyes on the girl who could have been my daughter. . . the girl who has been my child for twelve beautiful hours and wonder how they could ever have found Alice Connolly.

A rap of knuckles on the glass pane shocks a loud squeal from me, so lost am I in what should have been.

"Ms Connolly." The woman's voice is firm, but not threatening. "It's the police."

My mind races through options, or at least tries to. There *are* none. On the fourth floor, there's only one way in or out of my apartment. No one was ever supposed to connect any of this to Alice Connolly. I can't risk a confrontation with Caitlin here. I do the only thing I can.

A sob throbs me, jerking my body like the cry of a child does.

It's over.

My throat constricts tightly, but I manage to croak a reply.

"Be right there, officers."

33

"Thanks for coming along, officers," Kathy says warmly from the rear seat of the car.

Constables Karen Bennett and Paul Gallagher grin from the front seat. Both officers are quite happy to accompany her. Bennett, a candidate for CID, has been bending Kathy's ear about preparing for the interviews for almost the entire journey.

"You're welcome, ma'am," she smiles from the front passenger seat.

Having eliminated three of the women as suspects, Steve and young Gilmour are in Fife interviewing another from Blythe's list. Kathy's pick is the most likely of all of them to be Alice Kinney in a new life. She's a match on almost all of the criteria: height, age, eye colour and build. She also works in the banking sector.

"Just at the end of this street, Karen," Gallagher directs his partner.

Pulling the unmarked unit in behind an overfull skip, Karen is the last to exit the vehicle, joining Kathy and her partner at the entrance to an upmarket apartment in the West End of the City.

"Number 14/4," Kathy reads from her notes. "We're here to interview a woman in her late forties about a historic case. Depending on her answers we may have to take her into custody. The Sherriff has issued us a warrant granting us permission to take blood and run a DNA test, if required."

The young uniformed officers nod along.

"I'd appreciate it if you two could initiate contact. As uniformed officers, it would be best if you made the introductions."

Gallagher and Bennett lead the way into the apartment block, Kathy following behind. It's an old Georgian block, all big windows, high ceilings and large apartments. Expensive.

As they reach the end of the hall, Bennett turns to address Kathy. "Bit of luck, ma'am. There's a lift."

"Don't come across that often in these types of buildings," Kathy says.

Bennett smiles in reply and jabs a finger onto the button to call the lift.

Emerging onto the fourth-floor balcony, Kathy hangs back, allowing the uniformed officers to take the lead. Approaching a frosted glass door, marked as number 14, Bennett gives the toughened glass a classic polis-knock; hard enough to alert, with just a hint of threat.

A few silent moments later, a voice calls back from inside, "Be right there, officers."

The door opens inward, pulled by an electric motor revealing a middle-aged woman with a kindly face and inquisitive look, gazing up at them from her wheelchair.

"How can I help you, officers?" she asks pleasantly.

Kathy steps into view. "Good morning, Mrs Lamond. I'm Detective Inspector McGuire. I'm here to interview you as I'm hoping you can assist on an historic case I'm working on."

"Sure, come on in," Mrs Lamond says cheerily, a hint of a Texan accent. With a jerk on the little joystick, she whirls her motorised chair around in a tight one-eighty before leading them through to her living room.

Kathy's eyes move over the woman in the chair. *Not a recent addition to the chair, she's been riding it a while.*

"Have a seat," Mrs Lamond suggests, indicating an armchair to Kathy's right.

"I won't keep you long," Kathy states. "Would you mind me asking how long you've been in the chair, Mrs Lamond?"

Puzzled, Lamond narrows her eyes before answering. "More than twenty years now, Detective. Horse-riding accident back home, came here for specialist treatment I couldn't get at home and never left. Got married, had a life, all that stuff," Mrs Lamond smiles, gesturing absently towards the walls.

Kathy's eyes move around the apartment. Images from over the years adorn the walls and shelves. Kids, Mrs and Mr Lamond travelling, laughing, living their lives, like she said. In all of the images, Mrs Lamond is in her chair.

"Always intended to go back to the States, but never did." She shrugs to punctuate.

Despite the elimination of her most promising suspect, Kathy smiles. "Well, look, I'm sorry Mrs Lamond, but it seems I won't need to ask you any questions after all. You're clearly not the person we're looking for."

Mrs Lamond's eyebrows rise in mock indignation. "Oh, you don't think that I'm capable?" she asks playfully.

Kathy nods at the array of photos around the apartment. "Oh I can see you're very capable, Mrs Lamond, but I can also see that you're not a murderer."

Mrs Lamond's face drops. "You're the detective who's leading the Tequila case, aren't you?" she asks.

Kathy bobs a nod. "Yes, but I can't really talk about that. Look, I'll get away and give you your peace and quiet back, Mrs Lamond. Sorry to interrupt your day."

Kathy follows Mrs Lamond back to the frosted door, Gallagher and Bennett's silhouettes darkening the glass from outside. With the press of a button, Mrs Lamond opens her door.

As Kathy steps into the hall, Mrs Lamond calls out, "Detective? Not everyone thinks what Tequila Mockingbird is doing is wrong, you know." A steeliness has entered Lamond's eyes.

Kathy buttons her coat tightly. "Aye, I know," she says before leading her junior officers to the staircase.

Then...

34

Filled with kids, runners, moms with pushchairs, dads too, students lounging on the grass with portable barbecues laid nearby, cyclists, dogs and life, Golden Gate Park, so close to Seb's place, was a fitting location for our farewell.

The sun on my back felt good, empowering. I stood there soaking up its energy, watching the people go about their day. I heard Seb approach me from behind, long before he intended for me to.

"Hey, old man," I greeted him without turning. "You're about as stealthy as a rhino."

I turned to find Seb grinning at me as he crossed the path between us. The ex-marine's customary stoicism had been replaced by an open and obvious expression of satisfaction. We had seen each other only a half dozen times–generally whilst I was between training camps – in almost five years, though we had spoken regularly over the phone.

"You look good, Alice," he smiled warmly at me. "Hell, you look great, kid. Strong, peaceful."

"Thanks Seb. I feel good."

Seb moved to stand by my side. I looped my arm around his waist, leaning my cheek against his shoulder. His own cheek crowned my head.

"I can't change your mind?" he asked, no real hope in his voice.

I broke off from our brief embrace to look up at the man who had changed my life. This able, strong man who had rebuilt me, supported me, even when he didn't understand me or my goals and given me the closest thing I'd ever have to the love of a father.

With his guidance, I'd become a dangerous person. The person I desperately needed to be.

"I'm ready, Seb. Don't worry about me."

Seb sighed. "I don't know that anyone could be ready for what you're embarking upon, Alice, but you know your own mind."

Smiling my thanks at him, I returned my cheek to his shoulder.

"Thank you, Seb. . . for everything." Seb remained silent, choosing to squeeze my shoulder in reply. It was sufficient for both of us. Nothing else needed said.

Almost an hour passed before we broke off from people-watching and enjoying what was probably our last peaceful time together.

"What time's your flight?" Seb asked, breaking the comfortable silence.

"Three hours. I'd best get going," I admitted.

Handing me arucksack, Seb listed the items he'd prepared for me, holding fingers up to count them off.

"British passport, driving licence and National Insurance number, in the name of Alice Connolly."

I nodded. "Good to be a Brit again. Being a yank hasn't suited me."

Seb hid a smile, but ignored my remark. He never did well with sarcasm.

"I've created you an unremarkable but watertight credit and employment history. Your bank account has three thousand pounds. The remainder of your money can be accessed via the name and accounts you currently use in the US."

Watching me shoulder the rucksack, he nodded once, as though to steel himself. "You can become pretty much anyone you want to be, Alice Connolly," he grinned widely at me.

"Any thoughts?"

"One or two," I replied.

All joviality vanished from his face suddenly.

"Will I see you again, Alice?"

"Yeah. . . I began, but was cut off.

"I don't mean just emails and phone calls for business." His eyes searched mine.

I replied honestly. He deserved that from me.

"Seb, I hope so."

***

"Flight BA362 to London, England, is now boarding at Gate. . ."

The tannoy announcement shook me from a moment's reflection I'd indulged in whilst sipping at a coffee in the terminal. I would miss San Francisco, I'd miss the States generally, but home was calling. The task I had set for myself simply had to begin in Britain.

Five years was a long time to spend in exile from one's home island. I hadn't realised how much I loved Britain, Scotland in particular, until I'd found myself in land-locked cities and states far from the sounds of the shore. Those places seemed so still, so placid in some ways in comparison to the coastal lands I came from.

A coarse Glasgow accent drew my attention.

"Fuck sake, Claire," the man hissed.

With a sidelong glance, I watched the middle-aged man in denims, beer-gut hanging over his waistband, bald pate coated with sweat droplets. His wife's case had fallen onto its side, catching his step. He kicked at the small case, sending it tumbling a few times. "Stupid cow," he spat. Almost without breaking stride, he continued past her to disappear around the corridor towards my gate.

With practiced routine, Claire retrieved her case, not bothering to check around to see who had caught the exchange. Wearily she steeled herself then followed her husband to the gate.

Shortly after, with strong, purposeful stride, I followed them, my first potential target in my sights.

Now...

35

My face is puffy and my expression resigned as I open the door to them. The female officer is only slightly older than her male partner. Clearly his superior, she offers a hand for me to shake.

"Sergeant Black. I'm a big fan of your books, Ms Connolly," she says.

Yet another layer of conflicting emotions surge through me at her manner.

The younger officer leans in towards me. "Is everything alright, Ms Connolly, you look a little upset."

Mind racing with a thousand questions, I find the composure to reply. "I'm fine, officer, just haven't slept much."

A playful squeal from the bedroom draws their attention.

Sergeant Black smiles knowingly. "Rough night?" she asks sympathetically.

I nod confirmation, forcing a resigned smile.

"I should go get her," I inform them and head for the bedroom, mostly to give myself time to process what the hell is happening. With Caitlin over one shoulder, my right hand absently patting her on the back, I return to the living room and warm smiles from the officers which break into wide grins as Caitlin lets out a man-sized burp.

"They're great at that age, aren't they?" Sergeant Black offers, a consoling smile flashes sympathetically. "I didn't know you had any kids, Ms Connolly," she adds, her tone friendly.

"Oh, I don't, I reply." "She's a friend's baby, just helping out."

Black nods once, seemingly accepting the explanation at face value. Offering her hands, she asks, "Do you mind if I have a wee cuddle?"

Standing in my living room with two cops who haven't disclosed the reason for their visit, my heart still hammers in my chest at having been tracked down but my face shows a friendly air of curiosity. I go with it and hand her Caitlin. Black immediately turns to a mirror, showing Caitlin her reflection, amusing her and distracting the baby from whatever her partner is about to discuss with me.

As he approaches me, the young officer's manner is conciliatory. In a quiet voice he introduces himself as Constable Wilkinson.

"I'm sorry to have to disturb you at home like this, Ms Connolly," he begins.

Finally, my consciousness accepts that these officers aren't here to arrest me. The stark terror and impossibility I felt at having been linked to Tequila and tracked down have finally passed. I smile at him warmly, my eyes inquisitive.

"What's this about, Constable?"

Retrieving a brown envelope from a folder he's carrying, he flicks his eyes up at me to gauge my reaction before he speaks.

"Your literary agent received these a few days ago." Handing me the envelope, he checks over my shoulder to confirm that the sergeant has the baby occupied.

Opening the envelope, I find a series of pictures. Mostly promo shots or images from a Google search, each of them is a shot of me or a character from my books. Every single one has been defaced in some manner with either profanity or threats to kill me.

Wilkinson moves closer as if to comfort me, should I need it. Piling the photos together into a neat stack, I hand them back to the young officer.

"Not the first time we've had these sent in. Some readers get a little upset when the fates of their favourite characters aren't what they expected or wanted them to be. It's just an unfortunate consequence of having a successful series like the *Vampire High* books," I inform him pragmatically.

He nods once. "Yes, Ms Connolly, so we understand, but on this occasion the person has followed through on his threats."

"What's happened?"

"I'm afraid that your literary agent was attacked outside her office last night by the person responsible for these photos."

"Is Jess ok?" I ask. A slight grimace passes his face before he answers. "She was hurt quite badly, Ms Connolly. Two broken ribs, fractured cheek bone and a nasty cut to her forearm."

I feel cold anger begin to grow. I like Jess, she's a good person and doesn't deserve for this to have been done to her. Aware that Wilkinson has noticed my anger I relax my expression into one of concern.

"Did you catch him?"

"No, but we have a name and a good idea of where he's likely to be later this morning. CCTV caught the entire incident and one of our officers recognised him from a previous case. Most likely he believes that he's got away with the assault and will turn up for work later today. We're here to ensure that he doesn't come to your apartment before he is arrested."

Lucky for him.

Pushing aside my anger, I thank the young officer, insisting that I'll be fine in my apartment.

"Sergeant Black and I have been instructed to stay with you until the suspect is in custody." Wilkinson must catch a look from me as he immediately follows up by apologising. "Sorry, Ms Connolly. We'll get out of here and let you get on with your day as soon as we get the nod."

Wilkinson has a nice face. Kind, with quick intelligence in his eyes, he clearly likes his job. Black has re-joined us at the mention of her name. She too is the type of police officer who puts one at ease and reassures with her presence.

"We'll be outside in the hall, Ms Connolly," she says handing Caitlin to me. Caitlin reaches out to grab Wilkinson's index finger and shakes it. He reacts with a smile, "Well pleased to meet you too. . ." he waits for me to give a name.

"Nicole. Her name is Nicole," I tell them, deciding her new name there and then. "And I insist that you stay inside with Nicole and me. I'll make us some French toast and coffee, okay?"

Wilkinson looks to his sergeant.

"That's very kind of you, Ms Connolly. If it wouldn't be an intrusion?"

I wave off her concern. "Not at all. Nicole and I hadn't planned on going out until this afternoon anyway."

"Somewhere nice?" Black asks as we stroll to the kitchen.

"Yeah," I reply. "We're going on a little trip."

***

Twelve hours later

Hair looped up in a little pony-tail, dressed in a new outfit that makes her green eyes pop, Nicole rotates her head around choosing and following random people passing by in the terminal. She's the least discreet people-watcher in the world, eliciting smiles and waves from those who notice her observing them.

I blow a strand of my own, newly brunette, hair from my right eye, before taking an appreciatively long sniff at the top of my daughter's head. In my small rucksack, boarding passes for our flight to Bordeaux, new passports for Nicole and I, driver's licence and bank cards for me, birth certificate for Nicole.

Nicole Martin.
Mother: Alice Martin.
Father: Undisclosed.
Mother's profession: Translator.

I also have a few thousand euros, not enough to stand out as an unusual sum. Aside from my Christian name the only thing I've bothered to bring from my previous life is a little rubber giraffe I bought for Nicole, which she loves. Whatever we need in Bordeaux, we can obtain. Seb has begun moving all of my assets, as well as my future earnings from Alice Connolly's books, through the series of accounts we pre-planned.

Tequila is gone, at least for the moment, her last kill pored over by the authorities. The hunt for the baby, well underway. She, Tequila, remains ever present on the news channels, or at least her crimes do. It seems they'll never tire of discussing her mission, her motives and her crimes.

Good. They have five years.

As though sensing the dark thought, Nicole's hand strikes me as she's waving at a wee man who looks delighted to have her attention. I close my hand around hers gently, bringing it to my mouth. Kissing my daughter on the back of her hand, I whisper to her, "I love you, little one."

Tequila's mission can wait. I have a daughter to bring up.

Moments later we stroll on, making our way to our gate and our lives.

36

Surveying those assembled, Kathy swallows acid as she acknowledges the array of cameras and microphones, faces and logos before her. News crews from just about every country one could name stand, agitated at their wait. Their faces, accusing, hungry, are not comforting.

Kathy steps towards the bank of microphones intended for her.

"Thank you for coming, ladies and gentlemen. I intend to give you a statement only today. No questions."

Kathy barely maintains her professional veneer as the journalists express their collective disdain. Allowing them a few moments to settle, Kathy wears a neutral expression. When the din dies away, she leans in towards the microphones.

"Early this morning, responding to a call from a postal worker, officers and detectives, including DS Jackson," Kathy indicates Steve to her left, "and myself attended the home of Gavin Watson and. . ."

Kathy pauses momentarily, to allow her words to reach all present.

"Three bodies were discovered at the scene. Gavin Watson, his wife Jenny and their eldest daughter Molly, who had only recently turned ten years old."

Previously unaware of these details, a gasp rises from the crowd. *Even seasoned journalists can be shocked on occasion*, Kathy considers.

"Preliminary forensics suggest that Gavin Watson killed his wife and his daughter."

Once again, the journalists and reporters break their silence. Many exchange puzzled comments and glances.

A woman Kathy doesn't recognise raises her hand. The woman shouts out in a decidedly Australian accent.

"We were told this was another Tequila kill."

Kathy ignores her.

"The evidence indicates that Jenny Watson was beaten to death by her husband. The child appears to have been strangled by her father."

Fingers work across phones and iPads, relaying the news.

"At this time, the whereabouts of their one-year-old daughter, Caitlin, is unknown. An eye-witness has described a slim, athletic-looking female leaving the home with a pram."

Another ripple of activity sweeps the room.

"Using CCTV we have traced this woman and the baby to Waverley Station." Kathy swallows another helping of burning acid.

"Somewhere in the station the woman and the baby vanished. A woman matching her description paid for tickets at an automated ticket machine. At the time of the purchase, tickets headed to several destinations were bought. We have no footage or any other evidence to indicate where this woman travelled to. At this stage we must assume that this woman took the Watson's surviving daughter. We do not know her intentions, we do not know who she is, but we would urge her to bring little Caitlin ho… back to Edinburgh."

Three other journalists break forward. *Is this a Tequila crime scene or not? She only kills men. Has Tequila stolen a baby?*

Raising her hands Kathy waits until those assembled accept that she will not speak until the room is silent.

"We simply do not know for sure if Tequila was present in the Watson home. We are, at present, waiting for DNA and physical evidence to be processed."

***

"I'm sorry that it's come to this, Kathy." McBride's face is grey; he hasn't slept for many hours.

"It's fine, sir," Kathy says, handing her warrant card to the Super. "I can't continue in my role, not after she was allowed to disappear without any repercussions for her kills."

A moment later, Jackson's credentials join Kathy's on the Super's desk.

McBride does not look surprised by Jackson's resignation.

"Neither of you are to blame for this, you know."

Kathy nods. "With respect, sir. If not us, then who?"

McBride forces a smile. "You make a good point," he says sadly. "Full pension, for both of you. Don't worry about that."

It's a gesture, but an important one.

"Thank you, sir," Jackson offers half-heartedly.

McBride stands to his full height, shoving his chair back with the back of his knees.

Offering a shovel-like hand to each of them in turn, he thanks them both sincerely for their service, reassures them that here's nothing they could've done to prevent the Watsons' deaths. That they will locate little Caitlin.

Kathy McGuire and Steve Jackson barely hear his words. Even as they leave, McBride's arms around each of them, they exist in a numbed state of acceptance.

Emerging into the corridor, Kathy takes Steve's hand. "You needn't have done that, Steve," she says.

With a squeeze to his partner's hand, Steve attempts a conciliatory smile.

"You go, I go. . . partner."

Kathy grasps his hand tightly, then releases it. Smoothing down her skirt, she looks up at Steve Jackson. A jut of her head to the door before she speaks indicates her intent.

"C'mon then, partner."

***

Six months later. . .

"C'mon, Bobby, for Christ sake!" Kathy grins at her husband. "I think Steve's getting fed up waiting on you, love."

"Aye, well he can wait." Bobby wraps his arms around his wife, pulling her close into his chest. "I'm really enjoying having you around so often, Kathy."

Pulling herself in tighter, Kathy murmurs her agreement as she breathes in her husband's comforting smell.

"The kids are too," he adds.

Kathy breaks off from their embrace, keeping a loose grip on one of Bobby's hands.

"Yeah, it's been great, Bobby. . ."

"Bobby. . . Move yer arse!" Steve's voice roars up from the downstairs hallway.

Laughing, Kathy picks up Bobby's golf glove from their bed.

"Here, go have fun with your wee pal," she says handing Bobby his glove. "I'll be here when you get back."

"Thanks, love," Booby steps through the door, only to pop his head back through a moment later. "Kathy?"

"You forget something?"

"I love you, Kathy McGuire."

"Love you too, Bobby."

Seated in a comfortable armchair, in her living room, Kathy sips at her coffee and fidgets. She's kept herself busy since retiring, but running a household, filling one's day with recreational tasks is a very different kind of busy to her previous role. Bobby reckons that she will adjust, slow her pace to match her new lifestyle. Having spent decades at the centre of a continuously frenetic department, Kathy isn't so sure.

Reminding herself to sit still and enjoy a few minutes downtime, Kathy becomes aware that one of her index fingers has been tapping furiously on the arm of her chair. Stilling her hand, she makes a conscious effort to still her thoughts also.

Her phone, resting on the lamp table nearby, vibrates abruptly, shaking her from a serenity she's barely entered.

The green WhatsApp banner lies on her screen.

Flicking the screen, Kathy enters the app, gasping as the message pops up.

The baby is safe. She is cared for and loved.
Tequila.

Kathy reads the message several times. Relaxing deep into the armchair, she resolves to call her former boss, McBride. But not just yet. She has earned a few minutes to absorb and indulge a sense of relief that surges contrary to her police instincts.

Epilogue

Four years after famous author retreats from public life, still no word of Alice Connolly.

I flip past the article. It's a rehash of the one they printed last year around the same time. Old news, in every sense of the phrase. Laying down my iPad, I switch off from the outside world, and watch my daughter play with her friends.

Nicole checks back along the length of the lawn, meets my eye and continues playing. She does this often: she likes checking on me, I've no idea why. She's a happy, secure and loved little five-year-old girl, not a care in the world, yet still she checks on me routinely, making sure I'm fine.

With her friends, she runs in predictable patterns, playing some synchronised game they've learned in school. I'm the *adult helper* today. The parent who takes the group of kids from Nicole's class on an outing. It's really just an opportunity for the other parents to get a break for a few hours, but the kids love their time together.

Nicole shouts something in French which I can't quite pick out from the background noise in the park. Waving her over, she turns to roll her eyes dramatically at her mother's intrusion to her friends.

Clearing half the length of the Botanic Gardens in a flash, she appears at my table, eyes fixed instantly on my wine glass. She doesn't mention it, but I can see the disapproval.

Despite me drinking perhaps as little as a glass of wine a fortnight, Nicole has frowned on any alcohol consumption since she was around two. Only when it comes to me though, she's unmindful of her friends' parents' drinking habits.

Staring at the glass long enough to make her feelings known, she moves her eyes to me with a smile.

"Mama, can we go around to the other end of the park, where the pond is?" she asks in English. That's our rule, French for everyone else, English when it's just her and me. It's made her accent perfect in both languages.

I make a show of mulling over her request.

"Okay," I tell her finally. "But I'm coming along."

"You haven't finished your wine," she says, eyeing the three-quarter full glass.

"That's fine, love," I respond pleasantly. "I'm not really fussed."

Nicole beams back up at me.

"Shall we?" I ask, bobbing a nod at her waiting friends.

She grins at me. "Hurry up then," she laughs as she speeds away, not a single care in the world.

THE END

TEQUILA WILL RETURN IN SUMMER, 2017

Also by C. P. Wilson:

The Girl Who Sold Her Son

Writing as Mark Wilson:

Wake Up And Smell The Coffin (Lanarkshire Strays 4)
Bobby's Boy (Lanarkshire Strays 3)
Naebody's Hero (Lanarkshire Strays 2)
Head Boy (Lanarkshire Strays 1)
Paddy's Daddy
Lanarkshire Strays: Collected Edition
On The Seventh Day

dEaDINBURGH: Vantage (Din Eidyn Corpus 1)
dEaDINBURGH: Alliances (Din Eidyn Corpus 2)
dEaDINBURGH: Origins (Din Eidyn Corpus 3)
dEaDINBURGH: Hunted(Din Eidyn Corpus 4)
dEaDINBURGH: Collected Edition

Acknowledgements

I'd like to thank the following people for their support in writing this novel:

Stephanie Dagg. Steph is a wonder and I wouldn't produce a book without her input.

Very special thanks to Jayne Doherty and Gayle Karabelen for their continued support of my writing career and to Michelle Ruedin for her insights and enthusiasm for the project. Thanks also to my regular beta readers as well as Rowena Hoseason and Michelle Ruedin for their contributions to the social media interludes.

Special thanks also to my work-wife, Ryan Bracha. Ryan is a constant source of support, creative inspiration and general nonsense.

Thanks to Betsy and Fred and all those at Bloodhound Books (particularly the editor for a fine job of polishing my manuscript) for having faith in my project and for their enthusiasm towards the novel.

A huge thank you, as always, to my wife Natalie Wilson for unwavering encouragement and support. I wouldn't have written a word these last few years without your belief in me.

Printed in Great Britain
by Amazon